Sudhindra Nath Ghose (1899–1965)—best known as Sudhin Ghose—was born in Bardhaman in Bengal. He moved to Europe as a student in the 1920s where he first studied science and art history before completing a doctorate in literature. Though he spent his entire writing career in the West, Sudhin Ghose, like his contemporaries Mulk Raj Anand, R. K. Narayan and Raja Rao, based his work on India, drawing material from the villages and towns of Bengal. An impeccable prose stylist and a master of sprawling narratives which draw inspiration from myths, fables, legends and epics, Sudhin Ghose is among the greatest writers in Indian English literature.

Sudhin Ghose wrote journalistic pieces, a scholarly tract, and three volumes of Indian folktales apart from the work for which he is best remembered: a quartet of novels comprising *And Gazelles Leaping* (1949), *Cradle of the Clouds* (1951), *The Vermilion Boat* (1953) and *The Flame of the Forest* (1955).

AND GAZELLES LEAPING

SUDHIN N. GHOSE

SPEAKING TIGER

SPEAKING TIGER PUBLISHING PVT. LTD
4381/4 Ansari Road, Daryaganj,
New Delhi–110002, India

First published by Michael Joseph, London 1949

ISBN: 978-93-86338-22-8
e-ISBN: 978-93-86338-23-5

10 9 8 7 6 5 4 3 2 1

Typeset in Adobe Jenson Pro by Jojy Philip
Printed at Shree Maitrey Printech Pvt. Ltd., Noida

AND GAZELLES LEAPING

The Last Village

I

We called it the Canal. Others called it the Kali's Nullah. And still others called it a branch of the Holy Ganges.

It was a water-way linking up a network of canals and tanks and *jheels,* artificial and natural lakes, and expanses of shallow water.

Our School was on the bank of the Canal.

To the grown-ups it was known as the kindergarten of Sister Svenska. But to us children, it was simply Our School. And we were all proud of it, though it was a simple structure made up only of a large hall, a side room and a porch.

From our class-room, however, we could see the barges, the bridges, the railway, which carried only goods trains, the green fields and the *gold-mohur* trees. This view was a privilege in itself. But the school had other attractions as well.

It was off the main road which led to Kalighat, to the docks and to the majestic Hooghly river. The side-street which passed by the school was generally quiet except in the mornings. It was used only by those who lived in Rani Nilmani's Estate. And this Estate was like a little village, 'a Sleepy Hollow,' which had escaped being swallowed by that ever-expanding and all-devouring dragon, Calcutta.

Sister Svenska's kindergarten was mainly for the children living in this Estate, though a few came from some distance. It was open to all—to the children of the poor, of the wealthy and of those who were neither poor nor wealthy.

Babies, however, were not admitted.

'Babies demand a lot of looking after,' Sister Svenska would say. 'I have only Karin to help me, and here are some twenty children. How can I take in babies?'

Sister Svenska was Svenska-Bibi to us and to all who knew her. Bibi is the same as 'Honoured Lady.'

II

When Tommy Dum-Dum came to Our School for the first time, he was accompanied by Moti-Didi. As a matter of fact, he was brought in one of Moti-Didi's wheeled wicker-baskets. This surprised us.

Those wheeled baskets were Moti-Didi's pride and joy.

Moti-Didi was a washer-woman, and she used them for collecting and delivering linen. Call her finicky, if you will, but Moti-Didi believed in doing things neatly, as neatly as possible. Could she roll up her washing and carry it in a bundle on her head like other washer-women? She always brought back the clean, laundered linen, which smelt of dried sweet herbs, in her precious wheeled baskets.

We children were not allowed to play with them. In fact we weren't even allowed to touch them, except when she was nearby; then we could help her pull them. And that was all. To sit inside one of them like Tommy Dum-Dum was more than we could ever aspire to.

Our surprise at seeing Tommy Dum-Dum in the basket

changed into wonder when we gathered that he was a *Kafri*, that is to say, a Negro, and he came from Demerara. We had never seen a Negro before.

'Moti-Didi is quite right,' I said to the others. 'She is quite right to bring the new boy in her wheeled basket. He comes from Demerara. He has perhaps never seen an elephant. Suppose he came across our elephant on his way to school? The elephant would certainly have frightened him.'

'And what about the buffaloes?' someone remarked. 'Do you think he has seen buffaloes either? Those buffaloes frighten us and they would have frightened him too.'

It was generally agreed that Moti-Didi was perfectly justified in showing Tommy Dum-Dum exceptional consideration and in placing him in one of her much coveted wheeled baskets.

'Otherwise he might not have come to Our School.' This was the view of the class.

~

Sister Svenska hunted for her spectacles as she listened to Moti-Didi. Or perhaps she was not listening at all. She was too busy looking for her glasses.

'No, Moti,' Sister Svenska said. 'No, Moti. We can't have the baby here. You know very well we have only children here, and not babies.'

Moti-Didi started drying her eyes with the corner of her *saree.*

We felt sorry for her. We liked her and she liked us too. But to be truthful, we were more sorry for ourselves. A Negro boy, brought in Moti-Didi's basket, and then not to be admitted to Our School! It was sad.

'I know, Moti,' Sister Svenska went on, 'I know you are fond of children. So am I. But we can't take in babies here. Karin and I have our hands full. I don't think we would be able to manage a baby that cannot even walk. Who would take him back home?'

'Take him back home?' exclaimed Moti-Didi. She seemed to be surprised at such a question. 'Take him back home? Why! I will take him back home. And bring him to school, too,' Moti-Didi added.

She gave a smile.

Sister Svenska, however, showed no sign either of approval or of disapproval. She turned her eyes on Tommy.

'Have a good look at him, Svenska-Bibi,' Moti-Didi went on. 'Have a good look. Tommy Dum-Dum is not a baby, but a boy, a grown-up boy. You should see him running after his father. A baby indeed!'

We noticed Svenska-Bibi smiling at Tommy Dum-Dum. Moti-Didi noticed it too, and felt assured.

'Tommy Dum-Dum is as strong as a bull,' Moti-Didi added, after a moment's reflection. 'As strong as a bull. He chases the ducks and the geese all over the field when I am doing my washing. And would you believe it? He is afraid neither of drakes nor of ganders.'

It was with awe we heard that Tommy Dum-Dum was not afraid of Moti-Didi's drakes and ganders.

If we could, we would have played about Moti-Didi's field for hours, and watched her put up the clothes lines, pour indigo in the vats, stir with a pole the contents of huge cauldrons which contained boiling water and soap mixture ... and it was good fun to run after the ducks and the geese. They cried 'Quack-Quack' and moved out of our reach, wagging their stumpy tails.

But those drakes and ganders! They were naughty! And they would not let us have our own way.

We were never afraid of Moti-Didi—she never frightened us.

But her drakes and ganders did. They would turn up from nowhere and chase us out of Moti-Didi's field. They would stretch out their long necks and run after us. They never made any 'Quack-Quacks' but a nasty noise like the hissing of the big serpents shown by the snake-charmers. Nasty was the word for them. They would make us run and climb Moti-Didi's gate to avoid their attacks. Mind you, it was some distance from the indigo vats to the gate and there were no fences round about to climb. Once the gate was reached and we were securely perched on it, we would cry out for Moti-Didi. 'Moti-Didi! Moti-Didi! Help!'...

And here in our midst was a new boy who was not afraid of drakes nor of ganders! The spirit of hero-worship moved us, especially the boys. We felt we would like Tommy Dum-Dum. I offered a brief, silent prayer: 'Lord! Let Svenska-Bibi change her mind! Let Tommy Dum-Dum stay with us!'

By now Sister Svenska had found her spectacles. She had two pairs of glasses, one of which she used for sewing and reading, and the other when she wanted to see what we were doing. They looked very much alike and, naturally, were always getting mixed up. The pair she was looking for was on her lap and not in her table-drawer. She put the spectacles on and gave a happy smile.

Tommy Dum-Dum was indifferent to all that was passing on around him.

He evidently enjoyed sitting inside Moti-Didi's wicker-basket. He was playing with a drum-stick and beating the air with great fervour. He scarcely took any notice of us. Or of Moti-Didi. Or of Svenska-Bibi. He was jumping up and down in the basket. At times we would see only the crown of his curly head and at times just a glimpse of his face. He had a thick, curly mop of hair and a baby face. His lips were very red and his eyes round. The whites of his eyes appeared to be extraordinarily white. His complexion was jet black, almost like the indigo in Moti-Didi's vat before she poured water into it.

He was happy with his drum-stick and his imaginary drum. He did not notice that he was the object of Moti-Didi's solicitations and Svenska-Bibi's scrutiny.

'Tommy,' said Moti-Didi. 'Tommy! Give *salaams* to Svenska-Bibi.'

Tommy stopped playing with his drum-stick, looked at Moti-Didi, and saw Sister Svenska was smiling at him. Tommy smiled back and then felt shy, turned his head away and slid down into the basket. He hid himself completely from our view.

Svenska-Bibi's smile was encouraging.

'Svenska-Bibi,' continued Moti-Didi,'you can't call Tommy a baby nor a boy. He is a little man. You should see him beating the drum when his father plays on the banjo. Why, he's just like a grown-up!'

Tommy Dum-Dum's head peeped out of the side of the basket. He gave a chuckle as he saw Sister Svenska beaming at him. Then he slid inside again.

Sister Svenska turned towards Moti-Didi.

'This little man,' Moti-Didi went on, 'will get into trouble if I don't bring him to you. The other day I was mixing some blue and, all of a sudden, what do I hear? A crash! And what do I see? My huge bucket of soap-mixture upset, my clothes-line brought down and Tommy sprawling in a pool of hot water with a ladle twice his size in his hand. He wanted to stir the soap-mixture with the ladle. Svenska-Bibi, I cannot always keep my eye on him. He is a little imp, that's what he is. And you call him a baby! Why! He is as strong as a bull. Whenever his father buys him a drum, he beats it so hard that it is broken in no time.'

'Where is Tommy's mother, Moti?' Svenska-Bibi asked.

Moti-Didi came nearer to Sister Svenska and said in a low voice: 'That's the trouble, Svenska-Bibi. Tommy has lost his mother.'

'And his father? Where is he?'

'His father works in the docks and is not at home during the day. Tommy feels very lonesome. So I let him play about in my field. But that is no life for a boy like him. He feels lonely and is always wanting to do something. Give him a drum and he will be happy. He will beat upon it all day. But he has broken his drum again. His father says there is no point in getting a new one. They might be going away soon. "A drum takes up a lot of room," his father says. "You can't pack a drum in a pill-box..."'

'He has no mother?' Sister Svenska spoke to herself. She seemed to be thoughtful.

'No, Svenska-Bibi,' Moti-Didi sighed. 'Tommy has no mother.'

'All right, Moti,' Svenska-Bibi finally said. 'You just leave Tommy with us, Karin and I will look after him.'

Moti-Didi was delighted. She was about to fish Tommy Dum-Dum out of his basket. But Sister Svenska said:

'Leave that basket here, Moti.'

Moti-Didi looked somewhat embarrassed. She eyed us with suspicion, knowing well that we had a special weakness for her wheeled baskets. Sister Svenska had, of course, no knowledge of this, and failed to understand Moti-Didi's hesitancy.

'No, Moti,' she said firmly. 'You can't take that basket away. Otherwise there is no knowing when you would come to take Tommy back home.'

Perhaps Sister Svenska knew all about Moti-Didi's wheeled baskets.

Sister Svenska turned round and called for Karin.

'Karin! Where are you?'

III

Without Karin we would have turned Sister Svenska's kindergarten into a bear garden. Not that we were particularly difficult children; but we were all fond of animals and would have brought our pets into the class-room.

Sister Svenska had a soft heart and might have been persuaded to accede to our requests.

But with Karin it was altogether different. She, too, liked us. But when she said 'No,' it meant just definitely 'No,' and nothing in the world could make her change her mind about animals in a class-room.

'Pets are all right,' Karin told us. 'I am fond of pets too. But the kindergarten is for children and not for animals. If you want to play with your pets, play with them. But you must not bring them into school. There is no room for them here.'

And Karin was very firm about it.

IV

When Mazdoor first came to Our School, he came with his white donkey and his uncle. We were told that Mazdoor's donkey was called White Beauty, and it was very fond of its young master.

White donkeys are rare. They were to us, in any case, and we hoped that Sister Svenska would let White Beauty stay in the school porch.

'The porch is not the class-room,' we argued among ourselves.

Karin, however, declared that she wouldn't have the donkey there, and Sister Svenska agreed.

Mazdoor's uncle felt somewhat embarrassed. He promptly promised to take White Beauty away and bring it back in the afternoon for Mazdoor to ride back home.

In an hour's time, however, the donkey returned to Our School on its own. It pushed its head through one of the windows and had a look at us. It did not notice Mazdoor, who was sitting behind one of the black-boards, and felt unhappy.

All of a sudden, it began braying most piteously.

The whole school shook. Heera became frightened and started crying.

'Karin! Karin! What shall we do with Mazdoor's donkey?' asked Sister Svenska as she tried to calm Heera by patting her head.

Karin knew the answer.

With Mazdoor's help White Beauty was lured by a few raw carrots to our play-ground, the plot near the trees by the Canal, and there it was tethered and left grazing. Some grey, brown and black donkeys were grazing on the other bank of the canal. They looked at Mazdoor's pet and brayed at it. White Beauty brayed back. There was a brief concert of braying and after that, peace.

Later on, Mazdoor told us what he thought about this braying competition.

'Hallo! You White Beauty! What are you doing there?' asked the grey ass.

'White Beauty wanted to go to school,' the brown one sneered.

'You want to become a *moonshee*! A learned one, a scholar! Is that it?' remarked the black and grey one which brayed the longest, and added:

'Eh? Why don't you say something? You, future *moonshee*.'

'White Beauty won't be allowed to come back to-morrow,' they all said, because, so far, they had not heard a word from White Beauty.

'But, Mazdoor,' we children cried in a chorus, 'White Beauty did bray in the end!'

'Of course it did,' replied Mazdoor. 'White Beauty simply replied, "You bet I shall be back here to-morrow," and the others did not believe it.'

Since that day Mazdoor's donkey gave Karin no further trouble. Each morning White Beauty brought Mazdoor on its back to school and deposited him near the porch. It would then rush towards the Canal and bray its arrival to the donkeys on the other side, and then, ignoring their return calls, would go on grazing by itself under the *neems*, the margosa trees, till four o'clock in the afternoon.

At four Our School closed. Mazdoor would then get on its back and return home.

Mazdoor was proud of his pet, and so were we. White donkeys, as I have already told you, are rare, and it was good to have a class-mate who owned such a precious animal and came to school riding it without saddle or reins.

V

Sister Svenska was looking as usual for her glasses when Heera came to school with her grandfather for the first time.

Heera was dressed in a white *punjabi*, shirt, and a pair of red *pajamas*, slacks, and she had a round little cap on her head.

'How old is the boy?' asked Sister Svenska.

Heera blushed and hid herself behind the grandfather.

The old man was somewhat deaf and did not catch what Sister Svenska said. Heera tugged at him from behind and he became as confused as Heera. He scratched his turban and pulled his glasses further down his nose.

'How old is the boy you have brought with you, Grandpa?' asked Sister Svenska, without raising her voice.

The grandfather stretched his neck. Apparently he could not get a word of what Sister Svenska was saying. He remained dumb, and this was too much for Heera. She burst into a loud wail. It pierced Sister's heart, and she called for Karin.

'Karin! Karin! Where are you?' she cried. 'What has happened?'

Karin rushed to her and whispered something into her ear. Sister Svenska jumped up from her seat and her glasses fell from her lap.

'Come here, Heera,' she said. 'Come here, my darling. Fancy calling you a boy. Heera is a jewel. Isn't she? A jewel.'

Heera stopped crying, but remained clinging to her grandfather and the old man became more and more confused.

'She is missing her goat,' Grandpa finally blurted out. 'That's what it is. Now be a good girl, Heera, otherwise Svenska-Bibi won't let your goat come to school with you.'

Whether it was the smiling face of Sister Svenska making amends for her initial error, or her grandfather's remarks about the goat, I do not know, but Heera's face lit up. She pointed her finger towards the door.

And there was her nanny-goat!

Uninvited and unnoticed the goat had strolled into the class-room and was busily devouring the contents of the big waste-paper basket near the door. One would have thought that she had been trained from her birth to live on nothing but waste paper. Soon she plunged into the basket and her hind legs were in the air. It was an exciting sight. We were delighted and clapped our hands heartily.

Had we met Heera's goat in the fields we would have given her a wide berth. The goats in our locality had a bad habit of charging us in the same rude way as the drakes and ganders.

But a goat eating waste paper and diving into a basket was a friendly sight. Rightly or wrongly, we assumed that Heera's goat was a good playfellow, and we applauded lustily.

Sister Svenska could not make out what was happening. She looked surprised and asked for Karin.

'Karin! What is that?' she inquired.

In due course Heera's goat, too, came to be tethered outside, near the spot where Mazdoor's White Beauty grazed.

This goat showed a strange taste in food. She did not care much for green grass, but throve remarkably well on thorns, odd bits of paper and orange peel. At times she would chew for hours a piece of dirty rag. But in spite of her curious habits she was not too unfriendly for a goat, and when we were in Heera's company she would let us rub her back.

VI

Bheem Sen's tabby cat and Ram Chand's pink mice do not deserve much notice.

These were brought into the class-room on the sly. And this we did not like. As a matter of fact, neither Sister Svenska nor Karin knew about the existence of these pets till an accident happened.

Bheem Sen used to bring his tabby cat to school in a closed basket which he had fished out of the Canal. We thought he had his luncheon in it. Ram Chand had a similar luncheon box, but it was of tin and had tiny holes.

'The holes are to keep the food cool,' he would tell us, and we believed him.

However, one day Bheem Sen and Ram Chand had an argument; over what we did not know. Then we saw them go to a corner of the class-room with the basket and the tin box. All of a sudden we heard miauings and there was a wild tabby cat running about with a mouse in its mouth! Bheem Sen and Ram Chand were chasing the cat and a number of mice were running all over the floor. The cat made a dash towards the Canal and the two boys followed it.

Sister Svenska was upset. This time she did not say 'Karin! What is happening?' She had her glasses on and saw all that took place. She simply said:

'Karin! Will you please see that the boys do not fall into the Canal, running after that cat.'

The cat disappeared for good. So did the pink mice. And we never heard any more about them. But Bheem Sen and Ram Chand were severely scolded for bringing their pets into the class-room on the sly.

VII

It was a different story with Seeta's duck.

Not only we, but all the people of the locality, had heard a lot about this duck. It was not a particularly noisy duck, but it was a clever one, and had two pretty rings round its neck. It used to follow Seeta about like a tame dog when she ran errands for her grandmother.

It had a funny habit of peeping into Our School—when least expected. It would walk quietly round the class-room as though on the tips of its toes and go out as mysteriously as it came in.

Occasionally it would make a few 'Quack-Quacks,' but that was simply its way of greeting Seeta.

Poor Seeta! She was so ashamed of her duck's mysterious visits and noisy 'Quack-Quacks.' She would blush and then shed tears.

We knew it was not her fault if the duck behaved in a silly way. Perhaps it felt lonely without Seeta and wanted to play with her. After all, how could she make her duck understand that animals were not admitted in Sister Svenska's kindergarten?

In a way we were sorry for the duck when it paid us its irregular visits. It came all the way from its home to Our School and then had to go back without even being stroked by Seeta. It was hard luck for bōth of them.

That it was a clever duck there was no doubt. We wondered how it managed to avoid the rough buffalo-drivers, the stray dogs, the bullock-carts, the lorries and the rickshaws. Perhaps, we thought, it got some fun out of trudging from home to school and then back home again, after a chat with Heera's goat and Mazdoor's White Beauty.

VIII

We had no liking for the buffaloes nor for the noisy boys who rode on their backs.

Buffaloes are such huge beasts. They frightened us.

I must, however, admit that those passing by Our School every morning were not nasty. They did no one any harm. But they were all clumsy and very slow. When they passed by everything had to come to a standstill.

The bullock-cart drivers were at their wits' end when they saw these buffaloes coming; the bullocks would become panicky and run helter-skelter trying to get out of their way. The dogs would start barking, and thus make things worse. Carriers with heavy loads on their heads were in a bad plight; they did not know if they would be trampled down by the buffaloes or not. The rickshaw-pullers would stop and stare; they were no better off. The cyclists would get down from their bicycles and try to find some shelter by the side of the pavements.

It was a good thing that there were hardly any palanquins in the mornings. What would the palanquin bearers have done in the midst of that jumble?

And those buffaloes! They simply did not care. They took their own time and trudged in their own fashion, carelessly looking this way and that, and now and again stopping in the middle of the road for no earthly reason! They never bothered about the difficulty they were causing. Occasionally one of them would try to turn back, creating still greater confusion.

The buffalo-drivers were as careless as their buffaloes. They were all boys, and they felt very important because their huge beasts held up the traffic. They would do nothing to hurry the animals along, but would go on chatting among themselves as though they were in the midst of the *Great Maidan* or the open fields.

Frankly, I repeat, we did not think highly of the buffaloes, nor of these boys, and it was a relief to see their procession come to an end.

One of these buffalo-drivers was a neighbour of Mazdoor, but certainly no friend of his. Maybe that was why we disliked that particular buffalo-boy the most. He, moreover, had a trained monkey. Would you believe it?—he had it dressed up like Mazdoor! It had a blue alpaca coat, yellow shorts and a red fez—Mazdoor's favourite colour scheme.

A dressed-up monkey would interest anyone, and we were no exceptions. But this monkey proved to be a naughty one. It was Mazdoor who first told us about its wicked pranks, and later on we came to find out for ourselves how right he was.

Once we found this monkey trying to bite Heera's goat. Fortunately the goat was too clever for it, and succeeded in tossing it right into the Canal. Of course the monkey did not get drowned, but it got a good ducking and lost its fez. 'That served it right,' we all said.

Another day, while we were watching the buffaloes passing by, Mazdoor pointed out to us that this wicked monkey was thumbing its nose at us! It was standing on the shoulder of one of those buffalo-drivers. We felt deeply humiliated.

We told Sister Svenska about it. But she was not much impressed. She simply treated the whole affair as a joke and laughed.

'Well, children,' she told us, 'monkeys will behave like monkeys, and play monkey tricks. I am not surprised. You just keep yourselves away from these buffalo-boys. They are rough and they use bad language. It is no use getting into trouble with them.'

From that day on we never stood outside the school while the buffaloes went by.

But the monkey did not leave us in peace.

One day it came in stealthily through the class-room window and made a dash for Mazdoor's fez. We shouted at it, and were amazed to find that our shouts did not frighten it in the least. Fortunately Bheem Sen produced his sling in time, and taught it a good lesson.

Here I might tell you that Bheem Sen was very clever with his sling. It was a lovely thing. His uncle had bought it at Hogg Sahib's Bazaar, where expensive toys are sold. It must have been a costly one, for Bheem Sen treasured it and used to carry it about with him always, night and day.

'You never can tell,' Bheem Sen would say. 'It may prove handy at odd moments.'

Though we doubted the usefulness of the sling, that day it did prove handy.

In his coat pocket, along with his sling, Bheem Sen used to carry a few walnuts that had gone bad and a handful of smooth pebbles. These pebbles were more precious to him than all the walnuts in the world.

'You can get walnuts whenever you want to,' he would assure us, 'especially walnuts that have gone bad. Just come with me to Hogg Sahib's Bazaar and I will show you rows of bullock-carts carrying sacks of walnuts. All that you have to do is to wait till they unload the carts and then pick up as many as you like from the street. You will always find a few sacks burst open in handling, and some which are simply thrown away.'

'But with round pebbles,' he would add thoughtfully, 'it is a different matter. Try to find me a round, smooth pebble that would do nicely for my sling. Something neither too big nor too small. You will have to hunt for it for days, and even then you won't find it.'

Perhaps Bheem Sen was right to value his pebbles more than his walnuts.

It was with one of his walnuts that he hit the monkey hard as it was disappearing with Mazdoor's fez. Was it the sight of the walnut? Or was it the sudden pain in its back? I do not know. Anyway, the monkey dropped the fez and picked up the nut, and then out it went through the window.

We saw no more of it for some time—much to my regret. For I must confess it was fun watching that naughty monkey.

IX

Though we did not like those buffaloes because they were clumsy, our friend Tu Fan took a different view.

Tu Fan came from China.

Some of us called his country China and some called it Cathay. But Tu Fan told us that it was neither the one nor the other! It should be called 'The Middle Flowery Kingdom of the People!' This, however, we all found much too long a name for a country, particularly the country of a boy with so short a name as Tu Fan.

Zahiruddin Mobarakali Ikramaudullah came from Dacca. 'If Dhurjatilal Mangelanarayana Thakoordas Pooroosotyamadas could come from a place called simply Dig, what business has Tu Fan to come from a country with such a long name?' asked Bheem Sen. Tu Fan said he did not mind if we called his native land China. Moreover, we could not pronounce 'The Middle Flowery Kingdom of the People' in the Mandarin way, which is 'Min Hua Chung Kuo.' Tu Fan could not help us much in this matter because he himself did not know how this should be done. Although he came from a place near Canton, he had left his country when he was very small and had forgotten his Mandarin Chinese.

'Blood is thicker than water,' Tu Fan's father told him. 'I understand why you have a fondness for buffaloes. They remind you of China. In China little boys thrive on the milk of buffaloes, and in return look after them and take them out to graze in the fields and to wallow in the tarns and rivers.'

No wonder Tu Fan liked the buffaloes just as much as we liked the red and black cows that grazed near Moti-Didi's ducks and geese.

Tu Fan had occasional rides on the back of the buffaloes, and that was why he had to be nice to the buffalo-boys and bribe them with bars of *rohat-lokoom*, 'Turkish Delight,' which he got from time to time from his father.

'This is all right,' we declared, so long as Tu Fan does not become too friendly with the buffalo-boy who owns that naughty monkey.'

After all, we were not quite so foolish as to forget that a boy could be home-sick. Few of us were born in Rani Nilmani's Estate, and Calcutta was a strange town to most of us. Did we not all feel like Tu Fan at one time or another?

Take my case. I was certainly happy at Sister Svenska's kindergarten, and I found Rani Nilmani's Estate very attractive. The Canal, the *jheels*, the barges, the railway trains, the lorries, the rickshaws, the gas lamps and electric lights, the steamers, the cranes with their clanking iron chains and huge hooks, and the sound of factory sirens by the dockyards, and very many other things close to Our School, were interesting and exciting.

But at night, before dropping to sleep, I would long for the familiar touches of my native village: the lullaby of the evening breeze to the yielding bamboos; the shrill chorus of the sleepless cicadas; the haunting strain of the goat-herd's reed-flute; the unending dance of the fire-flies; the soothing fragrance of the tuberoses and *hasnuhanahs*; the lingering moon over the thatched cottages, and the star-dusted sky of sapphire and amaranth....

Oh! What would I not have given to steal back to my village in the quiet of the night....

I could well understand Tu Fan's parting with his precious bars of sweets for the privilege of riding on those buffaloes which reminded him of his village in far-off China.

Tu Fan's liking for the buffaloes came gradually to affect me.

I found myself occasionally talking to these huge animals as they lay wallowing in a branch of the Canal. I would sit among the tall reeds, make sure that there were no grown-ups about, and then have a talk with them.

'You are not as bad as those naughty boys who throw stones,' I would say. 'No. You are not like those who go out birds-nesting. Are you? What is wrong with you is simply your slowness. You do hold up the traffic in the morning. That's what I don't like. Just think for yourselves what it would look like if all the carriers dropped their loads as you came along. That would be a fine mess! You know some of the bullocks are afraid of you. Instead of hurrying along and making way for others, you seem to enjoy lingering. And that is not nice....

'There are buffaloes in my village too, just as in Tu Fan's village.

'They are all right. They don't frighten anyone.

'You are all right too. But please don't be slow as you pass Our School in the morning.'

X

The only animal allowed inside Our School was Raden, a striped tiger from Malaya. It was bought in Singapore and belonged to Soetomo, whose home was in Java. Soetomo came to school riding on Raden's back, and Raden was parked in the porch till four in the afternoon.

Raden was not a living tiger, but a tricycle on tiny wheels.

'From a distance,' Soetomo would say, 'from a distance, Raden looks exactly like a real tiger, though not quite as big as the ones in the zoo.'

'But big enough,' we would assure him, 'to carry any one of us on his back. What would you do with a bigger tiger?'

It was tacitly agreed that we would never refer to Raden as a tricycle. Raden was 'Soetomo's tiger' to us. But not only to us; even the grown-ups called it the tame tiger of Soetomo, the boy from Java.

Raden's stripes were, I am afraid, somewhat original; you would not find such a pattern of curious streaks on any tiger's back in the Calcutta Zoo.

'But there is nothing strange about Raden's stripes,' Soetomo explained to us. 'Mother says Raden comes from Malaya. And animals there are very different from those in Bengal.'

On his way to school Soetomo had to pass Moti-Didi's field, and at times he would stop near her gate and call out to her.

'Moti-Didi! Moti-Didi! Please come out and see. Raden is a little breathless.'

Moti-Didi would stop her washing and greet him:

'How are you, Little Son? How is your tiger?'

'I am all right, thank you, Moti-Didi. But Raden looks somewhat breathless.'

'Let him rest while I fetch something for you,' Moti-Didi would say and would disappear for a minute. She would return with some fruit and ask: 'What's wrong with the tiger?'

'He is getting thin. He did not take any of the straw I left for him last night,' Soetomo would observe gravely.

'Is that so? Let me feel his stomach.' She would then wipe her fingers on her *saree* and squeeze the tricycle and squeeze Soetomo as well. She would shake her head and say:

'Both of you not only look thin but feel thin. That's no good. Your tiger is not too bad. But it is you, my Little Son, it is you who look thin and feel thin. Now here are two mangoes for you. Eat them at mid-day. Mangoes will do you good.'

'Thank you, Moti-Didi. Raden, too, would like to thank you;

but he cannot speak when someone is about. So I thank you for Raden as well. I am sure he would love your mango. I will put one of your mangoes with his straw when I put him to bed. He will eat it during the night. He is a bit shy.'

'Shy?' Moti-Didi would express great surprise. 'Shy? Is he? He is not a newly-wedded bridegroom! What business has a tiger to be shy? And a striped tiger, at that?'

Soetomo had no answer for such questions.

'Do you know, Moti-Didi,' he would finally say, 'when it is very dark and no one is about, Raden jumps out through the window. He crosses the Canal, the railway lines, the waterways, and the Ganges, and comes back just in time when the sun rises. I think he has been running about too much, and that is why he has become thin. Your mango will do him good, I am sure.'

'A tiger is a tiger,' Moti-Didi would reason. 'That is what I say. Of course he will jump about. He can't help it. Can he? But the mangoes are for you, my Little Son. You eat both of them and leave the stones for your tiger with his straw. He will munch the stones all right at night time, when no one is watching him. A tiger cannot eat fruit-pulp, and it is no good offering him a whole mango.'

'I will give him the stones then,' Soetomo would acquiesce. 'But what shall I do if he comes out through the window at night time and frightens your ducks and geese and fights with your drakes and ganders?'

'Oh! That's easy to stop.' Moti-Didi would lower her voice as though she would not like anyone to overhear her giving away a secret. 'That's easy to stop. You just tie him up with a stout piece of string before you go to bed. Tie him up. Then he won't be able to jump out through the window and frighten my poor fowls....

'Now, my Little Son, I must be getting along with my work. Tell your mother I shall fetch her washing at midday to-morrow.

And don't forget to eat those mangoes at tiffin-time, when you have your mid-day snack.'

XI

Sometimes Soetomo would stop at the wheelwright's workshop on his way to school.

The wheelwright was also the blacksmith and the tinker of our locality. He and his apprentices did all sorts of odd jobs—plumbing, carpentry, cabinet-making, forging pots and pans, overhauling carriages and carts, repairing boats and barges, and a hundred other things. The things that he did not undertake would make a shorter list than those he did.

He was, however, called the wheelwright, because of an enormous cart-wheel, precariously suspended from a rather slender pole, which decorated the entrance to his workshop. This wheel had been painted in gold ages ago, and most of the paint was nearly gone. Some flakes, however, still adorned it with irregular patterns.

We could not imagine a wizard's cavern more fascinating than our wheelwright's workshop. Its furnaces, a big one and some smaller ones, were a great attraction. What interested us most about these furnaces was the intense glow the coals gave when the bellows worked. It was also engrossing to watch the red hot metal bars hammered into shape. Cascades of sparks flew as from a fountain of fire. It was like fireworks at the Dewalee festival! It took our breath away to see the bullocks shod with iron hoofs and the cart-wheels fitted with iron bands and then dipped into water. How the sizzling steam came out—vapour coloured by the light of the furnaces! Some of the wheelwright's apprentices used blow-pipes. These, too, were interesting. But we were never allowed to approach them. Had we had the chance we would have spent hours in that workshop. To watch things being made, we decided, was even greater fun than running after Moti-Didi's ducks and geese.... That place cast a spell over us, and we thought the wheelwright greater than any fairytale magician.

That was why, in spite of the huge cart-wheel hanging over the entrance to the workshop, we would peep in whenever we could, and try to engage the wheelwright in conversation. We called him 'Cha-Cha'; that is to say, 'our Moslem Uncle.'

But that cart-wheel dangling overhead! How we hated it. There was no knowing when the pole might suddenly crack or the rusty chain snap, the chain that tied the wheel to the pole! We children often speculated among ourselves on the heaviness of that ungainly shop sign. We even hinted to the kind wheelwright that he might get rid of the menace. What good did that gigantic cart-wheel do hanging above the entrance? Apparently the wheelwright found it attractive. He took no notice of our discreet suggestions.

'Are you not afraid, Cha-Cha?' I asked him one day as he was sitting under his shop-sign. 'Are you not afraid that this cart-wheel might one day fall on you and maim you or even kill you?'

'A wheelwright killed by his own wheel?' Cha-Cha laughed loudly. 'That would be news! It is the model of the biggest wheel I have ever made. It is nearly as big as the wheels of the Car of Juggernath at Puri.'

This piece of information gave me no consolation.

Of course we could not possibly tell him: 'Please take that eye-sore away. Burn it, if you will, and make the entrance to your workshop safe for us and for everyone.' That would not have been polite. He might have taken offence. Evidently he was proud of the wheel and was not concerned with our obsession.

The mere fact that he allowed us to cross the threshold of his shop when we had no business there was a high privilege. And appreciated. How could we shamelessly ask him to destroy what he regarded as his masterpiece?

Yet in our prayers we would at times ask for the destruction of that shop sign, particularly on windy nights. We hoped and prayed that the god of the wind would kindly blow that heavy thing off its perch in the middle of the night, whisk it away like a feather and land it somewhere far off, right in the middle of the pool, say, where the buffaloes wallowed. That would stop Cha-Cha from retrieving it. We did not want anyone to get hurt nor did we want to hurt the feelings of the wheelwright. But we had to think of ourselves too. It would have been such a relief if only the wind would listen to our prayers and render us a service! What good was that wheel? What use was that eternal threat of sudden extinction?

That wheel was a nightmare. And even now I have the shivers when I think of it.

Our wheelwright was a busy man, as you might judge from the examples of his activities. When he had a big job in hand he would not let us come in.

'Not now, children,' he would wave his hand. 'Not now. I would not like to see any of you burnt to cinders. Look in tomorrow morning.'

The wheelwright was, as a rule, less busy in the mornings. He would then leave the routine work in the hands of his apprentices and come out and sit on a *charpoy*, a tiny divan, right underneath his shop sign. In an unconcerned way he would smoke his hookah, the hubble-bubble, or would caress his beard.

When he smoked we knew he was in a good humour. And when he caressed his beard he was in a better humour. When he combed his beard he was in his best humour. We came to learn these signs of his moods.

This knowledge was helpful. We knew when we could stop and have a chat or ask for a special favour, and when we should avoid him and keep clear of his workshop.

'We wish,' we would say to each other, 'we wish Cha-Cha would smoke his hookah in the afternoons as well. It would be so nice.'

~

'How is your tiger?' the wheelwright would ask Soetomo. And then without waiting for a reply would add:

'You are not going to tell me that your tiger is becoming thinner. He seems to be growing fast. If he grows at this rate you will soon need a ladder to climb on his back.'

Such remarks pleased Soetomo immensely.

He would caress Raden's head lovingly and say:

'Do you know, Uncle, sometimes I find Raden has become thin and at other times I find he has grown fat? Moti-Didi tells me that I ought to tie him up at night time to keep him from rushing about. She says Raden may eat mango-stones.'

'Not a bad idea,' the wheelwright would avow. 'Not a bad idea at all. Your Moti-Didi is full of ideas. But if I were you I would give your tiger some grease. Let me grease the wheels a little bit. Always mind your under-carriages. That's my advice.'

Then without much ado he would grease the wheels and polish up Raden with an oily duster.

'Try it now,' he would say.

'It is fine. I can pedal better now. Thank you, Uncle. I am sure Raden is happy to have had some fat.'

'Sure. Tigers are fond of fat, and your tiger will need some more later on. Don't forget to stop here when the wheels start creaking. Come in the morning. Not in the afternoon, mind you.'

XII

We would often come across the local Postman on our way to school.

To us he was the Peon-Dada. Dada means a Big Brother. To some he was the Peon-Bhai, or the Little Brother.

Peon-Dada, the Big Brother, was like a Father Confessor to us. We could tell him about our troubles, and he would settle most of them.

Unfortunately one of our minor problems he could never solve. We wanted very badly to receive letters and there were none for us. Somehow we felt our Peon-Dada ought to redress this wrong. His bag was full of letters. Could he not spare a few for us—from time to time? Only just a few! However, he treated this proposal as a jest. This we did not relish in the least. And we protested. We did want letters to be delivered to us in Our School.

'No use starting early,' he would remark. 'No use starting early this business of receiving letters. Once you start it, there is no stopping. Receiving letters means writing replies and receiving still more letters and writing still more replies. What's the fun? You scribble and scribble and scribble—for yourself first, and then for others. What's the fun writing for hours?'

We agreed there was no fun in writing for hours. It was not an easy thing to do. Moreover, to write a letter on a small piece of paper would have been a pretty hard task for us.

We wrote generally on slates or on black-boards. And these could not be squeezed inside a letter-box! If receiving a letter meant writing a reply straight off on a sheet of tiny letter paper, then it was an ordeal indeed. That was how we reasoned among ourselves.

One day Peon-Dada asked us:

'Suppose you had to write a letter, what would you write? To whom would you address your letter?'

This question took us by surprise. We had no ready answer for him. I was bold enough to suggest that we might write to Sister Svenska to tell her that we were fond of her and of Karin.

'Well, if that is the case,' Peon-Dada argued, 'then why do you not go and tell her so? It would save you and me a lot of work. First of all you will have to buy your letter-card, which costs money. Then you will have to write out your message, which will take you a lot of time. After that, when you have put it into the letter-box, I shall have to collect it and take it to the Dockyard Post Office, and from there they will forward it to the General Post Office where thousands of letters are sorted out. Your letter will be put back in a bag and returned to the Dockyard Post Office, and there it would be given to me along with many other letters, and then, at long last, I shall deliver it to Sister Svenska.'

After a pause, he asked us:

'Is that not a roundabout way of doing a simple thing?' We reluctantly agreed that Peon-Dada was perhaps right. Peon-Dada's parting advice that day was: 'If you have something nice to say to a person, just say it. Don't wait till you get back home and then write a letter. That is a roundabout way of doing things.'

'But, Peon-Dada, suppose we have nothing nice to say, then we may write a letter? We don't like the buffalo-boys. Shall we write a letter to tell them so?' asked one of us.

'I would never do such a thing,' Peon-Dada replied. 'If you have nothing good to say about a person, then just don't say anything, and don't write a letter either. You may one day need his help, and it is wise to be prudent.'

When Peon-Dada came across Soetomo going to school he would stop right in the middle of the road with his mail bag on his back and say:

'Well, well, what do I see? A young man on the back of a tiger. I wish I had a tame tiger like yours; then it would make things easier for me. It means a lot of running about to collect and deliver letters. Can your tiger swim?'

'I think he can,' Soetomo would say, beaming with pride. 'But he needn't. He can jump over canals, and that is just as good as swimming. It's better—you don't get wet.'

'That's right. You can't swim without getting wet! Your tiger will do nicely for me. I have so many letters and packets for the people on the other side of the Canal. Only your tiger is a bit tiny for a heavy man like myself.'

'Yes. That's the difficulty. But I am sure he can bear your weight,' Soetomo would say politely, and then add:

'Do you know, Peon-Dada, Moti-Didi tells me that I ought to tie a piece of string round Raden at night otherwise he might run about too much and get thin.'

'I never thought of that, Peon-Dada would exclaim.

Sometimes Soetomo would look very serious and ask:

'Peon-Dada, would it frighten you if you came across a tiger in the dark?'

'That depends a lot on the tiger,' Peon-Dada would say. 'If I come across your tiger I won't be frightened. I shall simply ask it to go back home and sleep by your bed. But if it happens to be an unknown tiger, then I am afraid it won't be much fun.... But I think Moti is right. A tiger should be kept indoors at night time.'

Then Peon-Dada would look at his watch and say:

'Well, Little Son, I must be off now. As I can't take your tiger away to help me cross the canals, I had better make a move. Give my *salaams* to your father. So long, Little Son.'

You may guess how happy was Soetomo when Raden was called a tiger and not a tricycle. We knew that, and treated Raden with due deference. Before eating an orange or a mango we made a point of offering Raden the first bite.

'Raden, would you care to have a bite of my *chapati?*' one of us would say and hold the rolled-up *chapati* in front of the tricycle. Then a moment later: 'No, no. Not too big a bite. Just a tiny one.... So you have eaten all that you want. Now I shall finish the rest.'

Soetomo would let us stroke his tiger, and at midday, when we had our usual break, he would let us ride on Raden's back for a few minutes. We enjoyed these rides though we were not allowed to go far—to the sandal-maker's shop in one direction and to the bookbinder's in the other—a hundred yards at most. This, however, was deemed a long enough ride for those who did not own Raden.

XIII

I have not told you anything as yet about Mohan, the Manipuri elephant.

He was, I believe, the sweetest of all the pets known to the children of Our School. Mohan was my favourite—so much so that I used to call him *my* Mohan, though he did not really belong to me. Sometimes I would call him Manmohan because I had an uncle who was so called, and he was much liked by all who knew him. My uncle Manmohan wrote poetry which was much too difficult for me to understand; but his friends would tell me:

'Little Son, when you grow up you will have to be as good as your uncle Manmohan.' So Mohan the elephant came to be named Manmohan by me. It was my way of showing my affection for him, and I kept this as a secret between Mohan and myself.

Mohan was a shy creature, and if he had suspected that one day I would write about him in a book he would have blushed to the very roots of his hair.

You may well say you have never seen an elephant blush. But then you have not seen Mohan. He was no ordinary elephant. Other elephants may or may not blush. Much depends on their upbringing.

I know of some elephants which are cheeky, thick-skinned and ill-mannered, and if you expect them to blush you will be expecting too much. If such elephants were allowed inside a bus they wouldn't make room for others; they would just stick themselves in the passage and prevent others getting in or out. If admitted inside a railway coach they would behave as though they alone had the right to use the coach and to open the window or to slam the door as it pleased them. When going out, I am almost sure, they would not close the carriage door behind them. 'What are the porters for?' they would bawl if you protested. In the streets you would find them holding up the traffic, breaking the queues, and causing trouble to all decent people. If they went inside a tea-shop they would smash all the crockery in no time. Ask them to behave reasonably and they would grunt back, 'Mind your own business.' You can easily judge them by the way they walk. Moreover, they are generally unwashed and proud of being dirty, noisy, vulgar and ill-informed. Mind you, they might be quite intelligent and clever in their work, but they are absolutely shameless and they never blush. They lack those finer qualities that make an elephant lovable and distinguished.

However, all elephants are not ill-mannered, and Mohan was an exceptionally well-bred specimen. It was a pleasure to spend even a few minutes with him.

In life we have at times to pay for other people's folly, and so it was with poor Mohan. Though his modesty and his good manners were inborn, I think the excessive shyness of his younger days was largely due to the rudeness of his neighbours.

Take one simple case.

No one could call the elephants of Professor Madhukar Babaji's Circus stupid. But that did not prevent their being ill-bred and hurting Mohan's feelings.

At one time some of Madhukar Babaji's elephants used to join the water-buffaloes in wallowing in the canals. There was nothing wrong in that so long as they did not hold up the barges. No one minded their being with the buffaloes in the afternoon, but no one took any notice either. This indifference of the public, however, made these elephants unhappy! They were anxious to show off and, if they did not succeed in attracting a big crowd, would go on making an awful row. Their grunts could be heard miles away. 'What's that noise?' someone would ask.

'Madhukar Babaji's elephants are at play,' would be the reply.

'My word! They are noisy. Aren't they? I never knew elephants could be so ill-mannered.'

'I presume they are all like that. They set a bad example to our children.

'They do. The sooner the Circus clears out of this place the better. Fancy sending children to Madhukar Babaji's show to admire those beasts.'

'I would never allow my child to come within a mile of an elephant or of a Circus.'

'Nor would I. Those elephants are worse than pigs.'

'They seem to be much worse than pigs. Pigs are dirty, but they are not as troublesome as these beasts.'

Imagine the reaction of a decent elephant to such a conversation! Won't he feel ashamed? And Mohan had to listen for weeks at a stretch to such remarks. All that he could do was to blush and hide himself. No wonder the behaviour of Madhukar Babaji's elephants made him feel more shy than ever—especially as he was very young then, and not forward enough to blurt out:

'Please don't think all elephants are alike.'

Later on something still worse happened with Pushkar Ram's Performing Pachyderms. Who Pushkar Ram was I do not remember. However, his Pachyderms were elephants all right, and big elephants too. But *what* elephants! Far worse than the noisy animals of Madhukar Babaji's Circus.

Within a few days after their arrival in our locality these elephants broke into a liquor-shop and drank up a lot of fermented rice-water till they became dead drunk; then they toddled out in an irregular procession towards the canals. The buffaloes were there, wallowing as usual, but their drivers were not with them. The sight of a number of drunken elephants frightened them, and they wanted to come out of the water and go home.

Pushkar Ram's Pachyderms, however, decided they would not let the buffaloes get out of the Canal. They even tried to climb on their backs and drown them. Fortunately the Canal was not very deep, and the buffaloes put up a tough fight.

This made the Performing Pachyderms change their tactics and start a fight among themselves. And to show their prowess, they pulled up a few telegraph poles and demolished a footbridge! Then they rushed through the fields bellowing with all their might, trampling down tulip-beds and rose bushes. And not one of these elephants showed the least sign of shame.

And my poor Mohan had to listen to more insulting remarks about elephants! Is it at all surprising that in these circumstances he felt like hiding himself in the remotest corner of the earth? Who could blame him for his desire to avoid all society?

Pushkar Ram's Performing Pachyderms succeeded in creating a sensation all over the town. A bridge pulled down, several buffaloes badly hurt, a number of telegraph poles pulled out, a toddy shop looted, a garage smashed up: these were some of their exploits. And who was to foot the bill?

The whole area—Rani Nilmani's Estate as well as the lands in the neighbourhood—were leased to the Sutasuti Advancement Company, commonly known as the 'SAC.' And naturally the authorities of the SAC had to take some interest in the matter. And in due course a Commission of Inquiry was set up.

XIV

They wanted to have Sister Svenska as an expert witness.

Svenska-Bibi was respected not only in our locality but in distant parts of the country as well. Her motto in life was 'Poverty and Service.'

This I did not know at the time.

But one day Peon-Dada told us: 'Little Ones, you don't know how lucky you are to be with Sister Svenska. She is a saint, as everybody knows, who is interested in children. The other day I brought some letters for her. There were foreign stamps on them, and I examined them carefully. Believe me, these were not all Swedish stamps! There were American, Swiss, British, French and Danish as well! So I thought I would ask Sister Svenska if it was her birthday and those letters contained greetings for her. "No," she said, "no. A woman must not give away her age nor her birthday. These are invitations to accept teaching work in different parts of the world. But I can't accept them." "Why not?" I asked her. "If I did, who would look after my children here?" she replied. My friend Doolal, who works in the Telegraph Office, tells me that he has handled scores of messages from all parts of the world asking Sister Svenska to take up well-paid jobs abroad; but she won't give up her work with us. Money is no temptation to her. "It is the work that matters," she told me. And how many, my Little Ones, will say that in these days?'

Peon-Dada shook his head. There was a moment's silence, then he said, 'Money is everything now! Isn't that true?'

We did not know what to say. Did we know the value of money? Did we know what it meant not to have any? Most of us had never handled a coin. We never received any pocket money. In this respect, the children of the wealthy were on the same footing as the children of the poor. Our parents thoroughly disapproved of our even touching a coin.

'Money is *not* everything,' Peon-Dada declared firmly, as though he were giving a very important piece of information. 'Service is greater than money, greater than gold. Though everyone is running after money nowadays, I tell you money is not everything. The more money we handle, the more foolishly we behave. At one time you could buy for one rupee eight *maunds* of rice, 640 pounds of rice, enough food for one whole year. And now? A sackful of rupees might be earned by mere trickery, by a smart one. But how much will a rupee buy? Try to buy me eight *maunds* of rice, 640 pounds of rice, and tell me what a rupee is worth nowadays. No, Little Sons, money is not everything. And I tell you nobody can buy nor bribe Svenska-Bibi with money....'

Tu Fan's father, I understood, had told him also something about the value of money and the price of rice.

'Do whatever you will, my son,' he advised Tu Fan, 'never become a writer unless you have some other profession as well; otherwise you will end as a rickshaw coolie like myself.

'At one time in Canton they gave me money enough to buy 500 pounds of rice for each of my essays of 1,000 words. And how much do they give for such essays nowadays? When you become a man you will find that an article of 1,000 words will not buy you even a pound of rice in Canton. This is what they call Progress! And Peace! Peace in Mandarin Chinese is "*Ho-P'ing*," which is the same as "Food for every mouth in a balanced way." What's the value of money and progress when there is no *Ho-P'ing*?'

I must confess we could not make much of these remarks on money and the price of rice.

But this much we did understand, that the Sutasuti Advancement Company wished to offer a bribe to Sister Svenska and to make use of her for their purpose. They wanted her to make some false statements and in return promised to make her the Principal of their 'Model School for Children,' somewhere near Diamond Harbour.

Sister Svenska knew about these moves. And she would have nothing to do with the SAC's Inquiry Commission. She refused to appear as an expert witness.

Then they invited her to become a member of the Commission itself. She turned down this proposal also.

'It is not honest,' she said to those who would call on her and try to induce her to come to terms with the SAC. 'It is not honest to serve on a Commission whose draft report has already been circulated. I shall have nothing to do with this Commission, nor shall I accept the post at Diamond Harbour.'

~

The agents of the SAC found that Sister Svenska had made up her mind. She was as firm as a rock. Nothing in the world would make her sign a false statement.

Later on the people of the SAC sent someone with lots of toys for us. The children of poorer parents were told these were for them if they would appear before the Commission. Only a few simple questions would be asked of them:

Whether the elephants had provoked the buffaloes? Or the buffaloes had provoked the elephants?

Whether the footbridge went down under the weight of the elephants or of the buffaloes?

Whether the children were fond of Chinese crackers? Whether by any mistake some of the older ones had tied a few of these crackers to the tails of the elephants?

Whether we loved to play by the side of the Canal?

And there were a few other questions of this kind. They all sounded perfectly silly to us.

'You are not going to bribe my children with toys,' Sister Svenska told the man from the SAC. 'In my kindergarten I decide what the children should have. I am not going to let you leave those toys here, and my children will not appear before the Commission.'

The man from the SAC said: 'Then I'll leave the toys with the children's parents.' To this Svenska-Bibi replied:

'You may try to do so. That is your business and theirs. In the kindergarten these children are mine, and I decide what is good for them. Outside the kindergarten, they belong to their parents, and their parents will decide what their children should or should not have.'

Sister Svenska then turned towards Karin and said:

'Karin! Will you please show this gentleman out?'

The man from the SAC became suddenly very rude, and shouted:

'All right, my good lady. The SAC will fight it out. You will be smoked out of Rani Nilmani's Estate without any compensation, and your kindergarten will be closed.'

~

Next day a couple of agents of the Monobol Assurance and Building Organization turned up at Our School.

They were all smiles! They praised our drawings and told Sister Svenska how much they liked the work she was doing among needy children. They even patted Soetomo's tiger which was parked in the porch … and told us that Pushkar Ram's Circus was insured with the MABO, the Monobol Assurance and Building Organization.

Then they proposed to insure Our School for nothing, and had an argument in whispers with Svenska-Bibi.

We did not know what insurance meant and what Pushkar Ram's Performing Pachyderms had done to the MABO. But we guessed that our visitors wanted some of us to appear in a Court….

And we were not mistaken in our supposition.

Sister Svenska refused to accept the bags of sweets they had brought for us, and their interview ended in the same way as the one with the man from the SAC.

'Karin!' said Sister Svenska, 'Karin! Will you please show these gentlemen out?'

These people, too, left the school threatening to ruin Sister Svenska unless she sided with the MABO.

All of us cried ourselves to sleep that night. There was only one Sister Svenska and so many men were against her! What could she do if one night they came back and pulled the school down? After all, it was only a frail building. It would not have taken a dozen men half an hour to pull it to pieces or to burn it to ashes. We did not know what to do for Sister Svenska, and even Peon-Dada could not help us in any way.

Next day Heera could not contain herself any longer. She threw her arms round Sister Svenska's neck and started sobbing bitterly.

'Sister Svenska,' she cried. 'Sister Svenska! Why are they so nasty to you? Why do they want you to leave this place? You have done them no harm, neither have we. Why do they want you to go? What shall we do without you?'

Very soon we found Sister Svenska, too, was shedding tears.

It was too much for us. To tell you the truth, we were not so much troubled about ourselves. What distressed us most was the rudeness of those strange people who turned up at odd hours in our midst and wanted to order Sister Svenska about. When they found that Svenska-Bibi wouldn't do what they wanted of her they became angry and called her a stubborn old woman.

True, we were all small children. But we were old enough to sense that some big trouble was brewing somewhere, and that these wicked people wanted Sister Svenska to move out of Rani Nilmani's Estate. They did not like her because she was honest and upright, and so long as she lived in that locality they feared there would be little chance of success for their evil schemes. What those evil schemes were we could not guess.

This secret, however, came to be known soon afterwards.

Peon-Dada told us that the SAC and the MABO had come to terms, and the private Commission of Inquiry was mere eye-wash. They were going to make use of the fight between the elephants and the buffaloes as an excuse for turning out all the poorer people of the area and putting up a new little town in the Estate. They would build a lot of houses, and the fields and the rose-beds, and the red hibiscus bushes, and the *peepuls* and the *gold-mohur* plants would all disappear! The cows would no longer graze near Our School, the buffaloes would no longer wallow in the canals, and Moti-Didi's ducks and drakes would no longer run about her yard. It was news indeed for us.

Later on there was still worse news. Our wheelwright received notice that he would have to leave the place within a week! Moti-Didi, the sandal-maker, the bookbinder, the garage man, and many others, too, received similar notices. Finally, Sister Svenska, too, got a registered letter from the SAC. We gathered that the SAC regretted Sister Svenska's inability to serve on the Commission of Inquiry, and had added that in view of the fact that her kindergarten was too near to the canals it was considered dangerous to have children there. In other words, she was asked to close Our School.

That afternoon not only we children but the grown-ups too, were in tears. At the porch of the school we found Tu Fan's father as well as two other Chinese, our wheelwright and his brother, the sandal-maker and his three grown-up boys, Moti-Didi and her sister-in-law who worked in a factory, Heera's father and grandfather, Ayesha's big brother as well as her mother, and a lot of others whom I did not know. They all turned up one by one at about four, and quietly took their seats on the floor of the porch outside the class-room and waited for Svenska-Bibi.

'What's the matter?' asked Sister Svenska.

Heera's grandfather got up, as he was the oldest among the men and they had asked him to speak on their behalf. He had a white turban and a nicely ironed white *punjabi* and saffron *pajamas*; he had oiled his *chappals*, sandals, and polished the brass stud of his thick short stick. He looked very dignified and more distinguished in his manners than any of those people from the SAC or the MABO.

'Svenska-Bibi,' he said, salaaming her. 'Svenska-Bibi! We have come here to say: God's blessings be upon you. We are poor people, and we are going to be turned out of our cottages for no fault of ours. We are grateful to you for you have saved us from dishonour. You have saved our children from disgrace. Those who own the land here wanted you to say that the children here tied Chinese crackers to the tails of the elephants and....'

'Nonsense! Just nonsense!' interrupted Sister Svenska. 'Who, I should like to know, has told you all these stories?'

'But Svenska-Bibi!' Moti-Didi broke in, 'they have asked us to leave this place. That is no story.'

'What about it? They have asked me to leave this place, too, and am I in a better plight than you?'

'We know, Svenska-Bibi,' the sandal-maker said. 'We know. But where shall we go without you? You have been a mother to us and to our children. We can't leave you.'

'Who has asked you to leave me? I have not. I am going to stay where I am and so are you, and that's that. I shall see who dares turn you out or take away my children.'

Suddenly Heera's grandfather swung his brass-knobbed thick stick over his head as though he wanted to chase away a swarm of bees. Then he shouted:

'*Svenska-Bibi ki jai.*' That means 'Victory to Sister Svenska' or 'Three Cheers for Sister Svenska.'

The cheers were taken up by the whole gathering. We too shouted '*Svenska-Bibi ki jai*' and clapped our hands. The buffalo-boys, who had become very tame since the day of the fight between the elephants and their animals, heard our cry and joined in too.

A couple of surveyors of the SAC and of the MABO were measuring out plots of land in front of our school. They looked up but did not join in our cheers for Svenska-Bibi. They laughed at us as we went out in procession.

One of them nudged the other as Heera's grandfather passed by them and slyly remarked:

'That crazy woman will be thrown out soon, I think. She has been trying to turn these poor people's heads. Has she gone off hers altogether?'

'Don't blaspheme,' roared Heera's grandfather. 'You are an ass. Don't insult a saint. A saint is protected by angels.'

How did Grandpa hear what the young man was saying? In the class-room we had to shout in his ears to make him hear!

'You are an ass,' Grandpa repeated, standing very erect and holding his thick brass-knobbed stick in a menacing fashion.

Grandpa's attitude surprised the surveyors. They were dumbfounded. How could they have expected such remarks from a poor old man who, within a few days, was going to be ejected from his hamlet for the benefit of ribbon development concerns?

'Mind what you are saying, old man,' one of them whined, pretending to be indignant; I could see, however, that he was afraid of Grandpa's brass-knobbed stick.

'Yes, young fellows!' Grandpa said gravely. 'Young fellows! I *do* mind what I am saying. An old man must weigh his words. And I tell you for your own benefit: Don't blaspheme. Don't insult a saint. Svenska-Bibi is a holy lady. You will never be able to turn her out of her hermitage. She will stay where she is, and we, her children, will stay by her side, where we are.'

'Just wait and see,' the other surveyor grunted.

XV

Next morning a letter appeared in the correspondence column of the *Watchman and the Morning Star,* signed by Svarna Sheekha Devi—our Sister Svenska—formerly of the Swedish Medical Mission of Kidderpore. The letter asked for information about the rights and privileges of a privately constituted Commission of Inquiry which wanted children of a kindergarten to appear before it to give evidence. It also mentioned that the parents of the children had received notice from the organizers of the Commission in question to vacate their premises.

The same evening the *Calcutta Harkara* published an appeal signed by seventeen Professors and thirty-one Lecturers of the Calcutta University asking the public to subscribe to a fund in honour of one of the most devoted and self-effacing workers in the field of Child Psychology, namely, Sister Svenska, our Svenska-Bibi. In this letter there were a lot of strange names, such as Pestalozzi, Jean-Jacques Rousseau, Montessori, Froebel, Rabindranath Tagore, Carey, Project System, Visual Education and others.

Of course I did not read those letters. How could I read English? But Peon-Dada told us all about them.

And it was from him I heard a few days later that there would be no further bother from the SAC.

'One of the Professors called on Sister Svenska,' Peon-Dada informed us. 'With him came a retired Major Sahib called Peter Arnot Sahib. Arnot Sahib is a collector of old maps and plans. He gave Sister Svenska some photographs and the Professor offered her some old pieces of paper. All these make it clear that no one has any right to turn out Sister Svenska or the wheelwright or the sandal-maker or the bookbinder or Moti-Didi or anyone else from this place.

'They also brought a bag of money they had collected for Svenska-Bibi,' Peon-Dada continued. 'But Svenska-Bibi won't touch the money. She simply said she wouldn't. And when they asked "Why?" she replied that so long as she could sew in the evenings she would make enough money to run her kindergarten and buy things for her children. "My work is my pleasure," she said. "Why should you rob me of my pleasure? Use that money for opening a school elsewhere." And, my Little Ones, will you believe me? Both the Professor and the Major Sahib knelt before her and asked her blessing, just as you and I would do. Before leaving her place they said: "All right, Sister, you know what is best, but keep this officially certified copy of Rani Nilmani's Will, just in case!" ... And Svenska-Bibi thanked them for their visit and the trouble they had taken.'

XVI

Now that last Will and Testament of Rani Nilmani was a very important thing. So Peon-Dada told us. It concerned all of us, the young as well as the grown-ups, living by the side of the Canal.

Rani Nilmani lived in the days of Peon-Dada's great-grandparents, in the time of the *Barrho-Lat,* Governor-General Wellesley Sahib.

'A long time ago, more than a hundred years before your time, Little Sons,' Peon-Dada explained to us. 'And Calcutta in those days was not much of a city. But Rani Nilmani was afraid that one day it would become so big and so crowded that her gardens would be sold by her children or by her grandchildren or by her great-grandchildren for money. And there would be nothing but houses and houses all over her mango-groves and green fields.'

We listened attentively to what Peon-Dada was saying.

'And she did not like that idea at all. She loved her mango-trees, her *peepul* trees, her *gold-mohur* plants, her green fields, her lakes with pink lotuses and white lilies and blue nenuphars and emerald reeds. She liked to see children playing about in the meadows and cows grazing there and buffaloes wallowing in the waterways and the swans floating about on her *jheels*. She was afraid that after her death her property would be sold and all these would disappear. She had reason to be afraid, for her sons were very fond of horses and of gambling. Those who are crazy about horses and gambling do not, as a rule, care much for lotuses and *gold-mohur* plants.

'So she decided,' Peon-Dada continued, 'to hand over her property to the Government on one condition. And it was simply this: One of her Estates should never be built over nor fenced off. It should remain the same for 150 years, open to all who wanted to cross it, and all domestic animals would be allowed to graze in its fields and to drink from its ponds and waterways, and none of the tenants of that Estate should be turned out unless they behaved cruelly towards animals or children or their neighbours.'

It was good to hear that Rani Nilmani's terms were accepted by the Government, and that we were living in that particular Estate which could not be fenced off nor built over.

'And that is why Rani Nilmani's Estate is an old village in the midst of sprawling suburban Calcutta,' Peon-Dada added.

In the course of time the lease of the property changed hands more than once. But the conditions imposed by the long dead Rani remained valid.

In a hundred years Calcutta grew and grew and spread over a vast area, engulfing and swallowing all the attractive villages round about. But our area escaped.

When the SAC bought the lease of this Estate, they knew

there was nothing to prevent their digging canals or building railways through the fields. But they knew, too, they could not fence off any portion of it, or unreasonably turn out any of the tenants. Nor could they prevent cattle grazing in the fields, and buffaloes wallowing in the canals, and Mazdoor's White Beauty nibbling grass by the *neem* tree and Heera's goat eating thorns by our playground.

But when the fight between Pushkar Ram's Performing Pachyderms and the local buffaloes took place, the SAC decided to make use of the occasion to bring about a radical change.

'After all,' some of the SAC people thought, 'how many people know about Rani Nilmani's Will? And even if they knew about it, they would not be able to prove what was written in the original Will. Let us now begin by saying Sister Svenska does not look after her children properly. And we might also announce that the children of her kindergarten are particularly cruel towards elephants. They tie crackers to the elephants' tails....'

But the photographs in Sister Svenska's possession as well as the officially certified correct copy of the document settled matters for good. That Sunday's *Kanti Bazar Patrika* published a full-page reproduction of Rani Nilmani's Will, and Peon-Dada bought a dozen copies of this issue. He got one framed for Sister Svenska.

'All's well that ends well,' said our wheelwright after carefully examining the photograph in the *Kanti Bazar Patrika.*

'In those days,' Peon-Dada commented, 'people knew how to write. Look at that handwriting! Each word is as clear as the Dog Star at dusk. If people would write as neatly as that, we in the Post Office would not have to waste so much time deciphering addresses.... It is good to see the Will of Rani Nilmani. Well! We had a close shave. Anyway, we are thankful now. As you were saying, all's well that ends well.'

Tu Fan said that his father, too, had bought a copy of the Sunday paper, and was going to burn a few incense sticks in honour of Rani Nilmani. He had also drawn with a brush a Chinese saying similar to 'All's Well that Ends Well' in vermilion on a scroll of paper for Tu Fan to pin up on the wall in front of his desk.

XVII

But I did not feel as happy as the wheelwright or Peon-Dada or Tu Fan's father. It was all right for them, they hadn't an elephant as a pet, and they could afford to laugh. But I had to think of Mohan all the while.

So far as Mohan was concerned it was certainly not a happy ending, but the beginning of new worries. The SAC could do nothing against human beings and domestic animals, but they could vent their anger on elephants!

As those of Madhukar Babaji's Circus and of Pushkar Ram's Performing Circle were out of their reach, they decided to wreak their vengeance on Mohan, the only elephant in the locality. It was very mean on their part, I thought.

~

After four I took a stroll to examine the new footbridge over the Canal. It was by the signal boxes with cranes on their roofs for loading and unloading the barges. Freshly painted in red and orange, it looked very nice.

All of a sudden I heard a sigh. It was a deep sigh, and only a being in great distress could have heaved such a sigh.

I turned round, but saw no one nearby.

'Where did that sigh come from?' I wondered.

Then I noticed Mohan. He was hiding himself among the bullrushes. He sat on his haunches, crouched up, as though ashamed of being seen. Mohan was sighing.

'What has happened to you, good old Mohan? Why should you sigh?'

Mohan did not budge. He did not even wave his ears in his usual friendly way. That was a bad sign.

'Are you hurt? Are you sick? Why are you hiding yourself among the bullrushes? Come on, old boy, give me your left forepaw like a good Boy Scout.'

Mohan remained quiet. He looked at me sadly, and I noticed tears in his eyes.

'What is wrong, my Manmohan? Why are you crying? Am I not your friend? Or are you angry with me? Why are you unhappy? Have I done something wrong?'

Now, at long last, Mohan gave his friendly sign with his ears and waved his *salaam* with his trunk.

'So you are not angry with me. That's good. Now tell me why you are hiding yourself among the rushes. You are not a duck. Neither are you Moses.'

Mohan made a further sign with his trunk, and then I saw what had happened to make him miserable.

There was a new notice board put up by the SAC. It stated:

RESERVED FOR DOMESTIC ANIMALS ONLY
NO ELEPHANTS
BY ORDER OF THE SAC

'So that is what they have been after,' I said to myself. 'This is the outcome of the visit of those ill-bred Performing Pachyderms of Pushkar Ram.'

I consulted Peon-Dada.

'Well, my Little Son,' he stammered awkwardly, 'I don't know if anything can be done about it. It is too late, I am afraid. Too late. That's the trouble. I think I heard the crier announce with the beat of the drum some time ago, that the SAC no longer considered elephants as domestic animals in this area. So Rani Nilmani's writ will not safeguard Mohan. He can't go near the canals any more.'

I was upset.

What had poor Mohan done to be debarred from going near the canals? Our locality was his locality too. It was his home, just as much as White Beauty's home or my home.

'Oh, Peon-Dada,' I cried. 'Peon-Dada! Please do something about it. Mohan has done no harm. It will break Mohan's heart to see so many new notice boards. All of them say the same thing: "RESERVED FOR DOMESTIC ANIMALS ONLY" or some such stupid thing. Mohan will die of shame.'

'I know it, Little Son,' Peon-Dada sighed, and patted my head to give me courage. 'I know only too well that an elephant can die of a broken heart. But as I was telling you, it is too late. Only yesterday I read in the *Sanjher Pradeep* that someone ought to have brought a lawsuit against the SAC for their insolently declaring that elephants were no longer domestic animals. Yes, I read it out to Mazdoor's father, and he told me the same thing as the *Sanjher Pradeep*. Well, Little Son, we all have the same view. If elephants are not domestic animals in India, what are they? Just tell me, what are they?'

I did not know what to say.

Peon-Dada shook his head and went on as though he was talking to himself now: 'Little Son, our elephants are domestic animals all right. Only the SAC won't allow them in this area any more. I am afraid you will have to part with Mohan. It can't be helped. I am sorry. But that is the situation.'

And all that time Mohan was standing within earshot!

'Peon-Dada,' I said, swallowing my tears, 'Peon-Dada, if Mohan leaves this place, I will leave too. Mohan is my Little Brother. I can't let him roam about all alone in the world. He is too young to wander about by himself.... I can't let my brother go....'

'Well, Little Son,' Peon-Dada scratched his head and whispered, because he, too, noticed Mohan listening to our talk, 'I must be going now. I have a lot of letters for the folks on the other side of the Canal. Be good and brave. Don't be too upset. After all, many things happen in life. Living means bearing burdens. Look at Moti. Have you ever heard a word of complaint from her? And she had a husband and seven brothers, and where are they now? She lost all of them in the twinkling of an eye.'

He snapped his fingers.

'Just like that,' he continued, 'in the twinkling of an eye. She lost them all. They were in the same boat and the boat went down to the bottom of the sea. Well? She is carrying on all the same. Just as I said, in life many things happen. Moti is working all alone and does not even think of getting a second husband. She won't give you her right hand nor let you take her left one. Think of that....'

XVIII

So Mohan and I went to Moti-Didi, both very downcast. I tried to cheer up Mohan by patting him, and Mohan wanted to cheer me up by wriggling his ears. He knew I liked that trick of his. I pretended to laugh, just to please him.

Moti-Didi was preparing pancakes when we reached her place.

At any other time I would have rushed into her arms and begged for a pancake for Mohan. I never asked anything for myself, but for Mohan I did not mind being a bit too forward.

But that afternoon I felt sick and did not dash into Moti-Didi's kitchen; I stood silently at the threshold with Mohan by my side.

From the cottage opposite came the sound of banjo and drum. Tommy Dum-Dum and his father were practising their duo. They were happy. So were all the other people in the whole neighbourhood. Only Mohan and I were unhappy. The sound of music did not please me any more, nor the coloured lights from the barges. Nor the smell of the pancakes.

I was just saying to myself: 'What shall Mohan and I do? We have no one in the world. What can we two do? Where shall we go?'

Suddenly I felt Moti-Didi's arms round me. She lifted me up and covered me with kisses.

'You have been crying, my Little Son?' she asked, wiping my cheeks with a corner of her *saree*. 'Crying! What for? You don't love your Moti-Didi any more? Just whisper in her ears what has happened.'

'They want to drive Mohan away from this Estate,' I said softly. I did not want Mohan to hear the whole story over again.

'There are new notice-boards,' I sobbed. 'New notice-boards saying that all elephants must keep out. And Peon-Dada thinks that elephants are no longer domestic animals here. They will have to keep off Rani Nilmani's Estate.'

'Come, show me the notice-board, my darling,' said Moti-Didi, as she patted me on the head and passed her fingers through my curls.

'But, Moti-Didi, it is not *one* notice-board. There are scores of them. They have put up lots and lots of notice-boards all over the place.'

'Have they? Really? Then wait a moment. I must take a wheeled basket with me. You will help me to pull it, won't you?'

'Yes. You will see. Peon-Dada says that nothing can be done now. It is too late.'

'Did he? Don't bother, Little Son. I need tons of firewood for heating water. The more notice-boards I find, the better. You have seen my old broomstick?'

'The heavy one?'

'Yes. The one you can't lift. I am going to break it over the head of anyone who tries to take your Mohan away.'

~

Moti-Didi, the simple washerwoman, waged a battle royal of her own against the mighty Sutasuti Advancement Company.

As the notice-boards disappeared new ones were put up. And these, too, vanished overnight! Newer ones made their appearance, and they, too, went to make up Moti-Didi's stock of firewood. As a matter of fact, she succeeded in making up a huge pile in her yard.

The Sutasuti Advancement Company offered a reward for 'apprehending the person or persons responsible for removing the notice-boards.'

To everyone's surprise Moti-Didi turned up at the office of the SAC to claim this reward! To show that she was the person who had been removing the notice-boards she had taken a few with her.

'You are liable to be sent to prison,' the Manager of the SAC said. 'You have been stealing the Company's property.'

'Do you think so?' asked Moti-Didi innocently. Then with a smile she added: 'Produce your reward and send me a written note of apology. It is you who are liable to go to prison. Come downstairs and have a look. I have brought an elephant with me. It pulls my wheeled linen-baskets, and you have the heart to put up notices saying that elephants are not domestic animals! You wanted to frighten the poor creature out of its wits.'

'But that is no reason,' the Manager argued, 'why you should use our notice-boards for your firewood.'

'Why shouldn't I? Read this paper, and produce your reward. Hurry up. Otherwise you will have to go to prison. I have consulted more than one *Vakil* on this matter.'

The Manager read the paper Moti-Didi gave him. In fact, he read it twice. Then a few minutes' telephone conversation with the Directors followed, and without one word more he offered a packet of ten rupee notes to Moti-Didi and said politely:

'I have doubled the reward. Let us drop the matter of apologies. Please sign the receipt and let us forget all about those notice-boards.'

XIX

'It is a victory indeed for Moti,' shouted Peon-Dada excitedly to Cha-Cha the wheelwright as they discussed the whole affair that afternoon. To our surprise we found the wheelwright smoking his hookah at a time when he was supposed to be busy!

Not only Peon-Dada but the sandal-maker, the bookbinder, some men from the barges, the man who looked after the railway level-crossing, a few bullock-cart drivers and a lot of other people were in the wheelwright's workshop. Every one of them was in a holiday mood except Rani Vabani's cook, who was nicknamed

'The Old Chatter-Box.' She looked glum, and sat silently in a corner all by herself. She was watching the gathering with mock indifference. I could guess she was dying of curiosity.

'It is a victory for all of us,' broke in Ayesha's father.

'And what a victory,' someone else added. Others nodded approvingly, while 'The Old Chatter-Box' heaved a sigh.

'Moti is like Rizziah or Chand-Bibi' remarked Peon-Dada.

The wheelwright passed his hookah to the sandal-maker, saying:

'Have a *chilum*, a good puff, brother. And pass the hookah round when you have done with it.'

Then he took out a small comb from the pocket of his *punjabi* and rolled up his sleeves. We knew he was going to comb his beard. When the wheelwright had something important to say he would comb his beard. He knew the art of whetting the attention of his listeners. There was a dead silence among his eager listeners.

'Peon-Bhai,' Cha-Cha the wheelwright began gravely. Peon-Bhai, as I have already said, means Brother Postman. He looked round to see whether we were all seated.

'Peon-Bhai,' he said, turning towards us, 'do I not tell the young ones every morning that Moti is full of ideas?'

We all nodded assent, Soetomo more emphatically than the Others.

'That's what it is,' the wheelwright went on. 'She is full of ideas. She has already insured Mohan with the money she got from the SAC. But that's not all. The most interesting thing is the paper she gave to the Manager.'

The gathering was all ears by now. The wheelwright had a good look round once more to see the effect of his remarks. Our eager faces pleased him most. He scanned each of us carefully.

'While we men,' he spoke slowly, caressing his beard, 'while we men—like simpletons—were admiring the newspaper reprint of Rani Nilmani's Will, we were examining only the front part of it. The front page, I mean. We saw only the first page of the Will as reproduced in the Sunday paper.'

'And what did Moti do?' interrupted Peon-Dada, somewhat aggrieved. He was the man who was always the first with the news; but that afternoon he was just as uninformed as the rest of us. Rani Vabani's cook smiled at Peon-Dada's impatience, and gave me a sly wink.

'Moti did what only a woman full of ideas will do,' the wheelwright observed as slowly as before. 'Mind you, only a woman full of ideas, not every woman. When she went to Svenska-Bibi and read what was written in the Will, she examined the back of the document first. Teach a woman to read and give her a book; she will immediately turn to the last page to know the end of the story! And give you her opinion on the book! Moti did the same. It was the back part, I mean the back page of the document that settled it.'

'How?' several voices broke in at the same time.

'That's easy,' the wheelwright said with a note of triumph, 'simply because the back page contained what the lawyers call a codicil or some such thing. And this made it clear that those living in Rani Nilmani's Estate would have the right to gather, without let or hindrance, firewood, dead branches of trees, logs, etc., found in the Estate, and no beast of burden of any tenant could be taken or frightened away from its owner without justification, an adequate compensation and a payment of gratuity....'

'So Moti took Mohan with her and Mohan dragged her wicker-basket with her washing,' one of the bargees said. 'And she took those notice-boards as her firewood.' This bargee was a man of few words. It was surprising to hear him utter such a long string of words without a break!

'That's it,' Cha-Cha concurred. 'We men are slow. There is much truth in the saying: "A man thinks he knows, but a woman knows better though she thinks little."'

'It beats me,' cried Peon-Dada. 'Though I read a lot of papers in the evenings, I have never read of such a thing in any of them.'

'I think it is her name,' the bookbinder remarked quietly. 'It is her name that has given her ideas from her childhood. Give a child a nice name and it would lead a nice life all its days! The other day a young student gave me a book to bind. It was badly torn, and I asked him what the book was about, and he told me it was about a woman called Pearl, Moti, the Tree of Pearls, to be exact; and she had lived in *Misr*, Egypt, long ago. And I asked him "What did this Pearl or Tree of Pearls do?" The student said, "She was a widow who fought against the King of the Franks, who was a great king, a good fighter, and a holy saint." "And what was the good of her fighting against such a man?" I asked.'

By now the gathering was finding the bookbinder's story interesting.

'A widow fighting against a King of the Franks who was also a saint,' Peon-Dada said. 'What chance had she?'

'That was exactly what I wanted to know,' said the bookbinder. 'And the student told me that the King of the Franks was defeated, taken a prisoner by her and released only after she had received a large ransom. What do you say to that?'

There was a brief pause. It showed that the bookbinder's story was well told. The hookah changed hands; it was passed on to one of the assistants of the sandal-maker.

'We all know Moti means a Pearl,' the wheelwright said gravely. 'What shall we call her in future?'

'Let us call Moti by the name of this widow,' someone suggested.

"That would be a little too long,' the bookbinder replied. 'In *Misri*, Egyptian language, she was called Mamluk Shejer ed-Durr, the Tree of Pearls. By imprisoning a saint this Tree of Pearls committed a sin. So she made a pilgrimage to Mecca in a palanquin, and every year after that she sent a carpet from El Kahriah, which is also called Cairo, to Mecca to receive blessings.'

'My brother-in-law,' began the railway signalman, 'went to Mecca on a pilgrimage, and he tells me that even now a carpet is sent each year from El Kahriah to Mecca.'

'A pious deed is not easily forgotten. Its good effect lasts long,' said Peon-Dada, summing up the views of all present. 'Rani Nilmani died long ago. But her Will has done us good. The Tree of Pearls died still longer ago, and her carpet comes to Mecca even now. Well, in future, I shall call Moti not a Pearl, but "A String of Pearls." Moti-Mala, that should be her name.'

It was readily agreed that Moti-Didi deserved to be renamed Moti-mala-Didi. Didi, I may add here, means the Elder Sister.

XX

Moti-Didi, however, did not like this idea at all.

'A String of Pearls!' she gasped. 'A String of Pearls, indeed! I was born Moti, and I will die Moti. And if anyone dares call me Moti-mala I will break this broom-stick over his head. Your Peon-Dada deserves a beating, and that is what he will get from me one of these days. Having nothing else to do, he talks about women! Let him try to call me Moti-mala to my face and see what happens.'

When she had calmed down a bit she took me on her lap and said:

'What good deed have I done, my Little Son, to merit any honour? In life one should do what one can. Dry others' tears and make no one shed any. And ask for God's blessings.'

So Moti-Didi remained Moti-Didi as before, for us children as well as for the grown-ups.

XXI

From now on Mohan and I would go to Moti-Didi's cottage every afternoon and get pancakes.

During the day Mohan was kept busy carrying linen-baskets. Mohan knew the people round about so well that it was not necessary for Moti-Didi to accompany him always. He soon learnt where he should go and on which day, and in fact worked like a laundry-van. But he had to be fetched from the mango grove and taken back there. Somehow he did not relish the idea of venturing out of his retreat all alone, though he liked his work and enjoyed his pancakes.

And what pleased me most, he showed signs of growing up rather unexpectedly. None could call him a baby elephant any more.

XXII

Between ourselves, when I first came to know Mohan he was a tiny creature, not much bigger than Mazdoor's White Beauty. And for a long time he remained like that.

In those days it was really shameful how some careless people made unkind remarks about his size.

'Fancy an elephant about the size of a calf!' 'Mamma, Mamma! Look this way, a pygmy elephant is passing by.' 'What a funny little thing! Isn't it ridiculous?'

Many such remarks would be heard as I walked by the side of Mohan for our afternoon strolls. It was painful for me to hear such comments, and for Mohan it must have been still more so.

What could he do? He could not help being what he was—any more than I could help being a small boy.

Some people are cruel when they need not be. 'It is a grave sin,' Peon-Dada explained to us, 'to make biting remarks when they are unnecessary.' And what could be more unnecessary than to tell a tiny elephant 'Look here, you are insignificant, you are worthless, because you are not like others.' That was what it amounted to when people commented on Mohan's size.

These remarks hit Mohan like poisoned shafts, and prevented his growing up like other elephants of his age. He was shy from his birth, modest in his ways, and he became shyer and shyer, and more and more diffident. The more the people commented on his size the longer was the delay in his physical growth, and the keener his desire to keep away from men.

He was unlucky in certain respects. He was an orphan, and that was a handicap. Moreover, he was suddenly dragged away from his surroundings and dumped among people whom he did not know, among strangers who did not care to understand him.

My background and Mohan's happened to be similar. So I spoke the same language as he and understood him better than others.

Let me now tell you how Mohan came to live in our midst.

XXIII

When the naming ceremony of the 'first-born' was over, Rani Vabani's husband came to her and said:

'I have brought a surprise for you, Mother of my son.'

'What is that?' wondered Rani Vabani.

'Just close your eyes for a moment and open them when the surprise is brought to your side. It will bring good luck.'

'So be it,' said she, and closed her eyes. But when she opened them again they nearly jumped out of their sockets.

'A surprise indeed!' she exclaimed, and burst into peals of hysterical laughter.

'What has happened?' her husband inquired. 'What are you laughing at?'

'Where did you pick it up?' she asked, restraining her laughter with difficulty, and pointed to the elephant by the side of her husband.

'Pick it up? Do you think one picks up an elephant in Hogg Sahib's Bazaar? This one has all the eight signs of goodness, and I have been trying for ages to get a lucky one like this gentle creature. He is called Mohan.'

By now Rani Vabani had succeeded in controlling herself. She made a grave face. She looked Mohan up and down and pouted her lips, and turning towards her husband asked him ironically:

'Couldn't you get a smaller one?'

'Really I couldn't,' he admitted. He was slow in taking hints, and thought that Rani Vabani's question was put in good faith. He felt less embarrassed now. 'I tried my very best,' he explained. 'For ages I have been corresponding with elephant dealers in Assam, Mysore, Africa, Burma, Ceylon, Siam and Indo-China, and to tell you the truth I have spent a fortune in sending cables all over the world for the smallest elephant with all the lucky signs.'

'How old is this elephant Mohan?'

'He is about three.'

'Will you please empty out my sewing-basket and put Mohan in it,' Rani Vabani said with a grave face, while her husband looked confused.

'I think,' Rani Vabani continued sarcastically, 'I think a fruit-basket would do just as well unless you prefer the cat's basket.'

Her husband could not make out what Rani Vabani was really driving at. He was bewildered; he stared vacantly at Mohan and then started shuffling his feet.

And Rani Vabani had a new fit of laughter. She laughed and laughed till tears trickled down her cheeks. Everybody round her started giggling too.

'What are you laughing at?' snapped her husband. He was getting angry. 'What are you laughing at? Is there anything funny in my buying a lucky elephant for my wife? Is there?'

'We are all laughing,' Rani Vabani retorted, 'we are all laughing because the elephant dealers have made a fool of you. A lucky elephant, my word! A three-year-old elephant which is no bigger than a billy-goat! Would any man in the world but my husband buy such a tiny thing and call it lucky? You could have spared yourself the trouble of cabling to people in Ceylon and Siam and Timbuctoo and what not, to get a creature of that size. Do you think it can bear the weight of our baby on its back?'

'You bet it can,' replied her husband in a firm tone. He was in no mood to enjoy jokes, and did not find Rani Vabani's remarks humorous.

'Let us not quarrel over that. The baby's milk bottle will do for Mohan till he grows up, and when he reaches the size of a donkey we shall go out riding on his back—all three, the father, the mother and the baby, and invite our friends to stare at us. But that will take some time. They have sold you a dwarf elephant, and I bet it will never grow bigger.'

'I accept your bet. By the next Dewalee, the Feast of Lamps, in less than a year, Mohan will be double his present size.'

'Let us wager a thousand rupees.'

'Agreed. To-morrow a *mahout*, a well-known elephant-trainer, will come for Mohan to begin his training.'

'I'll bet you a hundred rupees no sane *mahout* will ever agree to train that pygmy elephant! And I'll give up eating sweets if he does.'

XXIV

That was the reception that Mohan got on the day he first came to live in Rani Nilmani's Estate. He was treated as an object of ridicule by almost everyone! Could you blame him for feeling unhappy? You know, no doubt, that an intelligent elephant understands human language in the same way as a man or a boy.

The next day the *mahout* turned up to examine Mohan.

He was a pompous fellow and bragged about the enormous elephants he had trained in different places and how marvellous all these elephants were. According to him everything big was wonderful! No doubt a large crocodile to him was a prettier creature than a goldfish, and an ungainly vulture preferable to a singing finch! I believe some of Pushkar Ram's Performing Pachyderms would have delighted him greatly. I do not know why such a man was invited to give an opinion on Mohan.

He looked at Mohan and started sniggering. Then he began coughing, and finally turning round to those about him, with a grin on his face, he said:

'I am very sorry, I can't look after that tiny thing, I train *real* elephants—the big ones only. This one is a pygmy elephant. It is like an African ant-eater or a tapir. I can't train a tapir.'

The fellow had heard about Rani Vabani's wager, and that was the reason for his rudeness to Mohan.

Would Sister Svenska have said 'I won't teach anything to Ayesha because she looks so small. And I don't care for Tommy Dum-Dum because he is from Demerara?' Of course not. All that she wanted to know was the age. She could not take in babies because they needed looking after in a different way from boys and girls, and she had only Karin to help her. She did not mind teaching us till we grew to be ten. But Mohan was not a baby in a cradle. He was as old as Ayesha.

The *mahout*, I heard later on, got a *bakshish*, a good tip from Rani Vabani. She was anxious to have some fun at the expense of her husband, and she got it. That might have been all right so far as she and the *mahout* were concerned. But what about Mohan?

The poor elephant felt depressed, and probably that was one more reason why he did not grow up quickly. Within a few months, when the Dewalee Festivity was over, Rani Vabani won her wager. This news reached Mohan soon, and it made him still more downcast. It is hardly necessary for me to remind you that Mohan could follow all the gossip he overheard.

Rani Vabani's cook was known as the biggest and the most indiscreet gossiper in the world. She could never keep to herself any unpleasant news. Thanks to her, not only Mohan but even the monkeys got a garbled version of the domestic quarrels and other happenings in many of the households of our locality. No wonder she was nicknamed 'The Old Chatter-box'.

It was she who told me that after the Dewalee, the Feast of Lamps, both Rani Vabani and her husband lost all interest in

Mohan, and he was left to look after himself in the large fruit-garden where the Omkarnath temple stood, just outside Rani Nilmani's Estate. Her report turned out to be true.

~

This huge orchard was known to us as the 'mango-grove.' Some one hundred years ago it was a pleasure park planted with many exotic trees. But in my time it looked like wild forest and was little frequented. A high wall stretching over miles surrounded it. No one lived there except peacocks and monkeys and parrots—hundreds of them, and a few gazelles and wild goats. All these were, however, most unsuitable companions for a shy young elephant.

Peacocks are wonderful to look at. Certainly it is a feast to the eye to watch a number of them trailing their tails behind them, and it is still more wonderful to watch several of them when thunder rumbles in the distance in the season of rains. A peacock in its glory is a marvellous sight. But the very beauty of their plumage and the sheen on their necks, seems to have spoilt them in an unbelievable way. They have grown to be very vain. To call someone proud as a peacock is to insult him.

What could Mohan learn from the peacocks in the mango-grove?

These birds strutted about in an ungainly way, and instead of singing they would utter ear-piercing cries to drive people crazy. Their habits were none too clean either. Mohan did well not to imitate the ways of a peacock.

The peacocks were bad enough, but what about the monkeys? The less said about the *bandor-loks*, the monkey-folks, the better. The worst features of all the animals of the world seemed to have gone to the making up of those monkeys of the mango-grove! They were unfriendly, dirty, quarrelsome, and thievish. I would rather be called 'Proud as a peacock' than 'Ill-bred like a *bandor*.'

As for the parrots, they are as lovely as the peacocks to look at. And in the mango-grove there were certain varieties which were even more beautiful.

I liked the red-tailed ones the best. A small number of these were first brought over here by the Portuguese sailors, and within a few years they bred scores of little ones. And in the course of time they became as numerous as the *nilkonthas*, and came to be known as the Calcutta parrakeets in my part of Bengal.

These parrakeets are exceptionally intelligent, and can be taught to speak exactly like men and to give messages by word of mouth. Strangely enough, the people of Calcutta seem not to know about the birds which have been named after their city.

It is said that a pickpocket who plied a busy trade in the Bagbazar area and did not mind looking into empty houses all over Calcutta, once tried to sneak into a cottage in Rani Nilmani's Estate. He was, however, detected by a couple of red-tailed parrakeets of a neighbouring household.

'What are you doing here?' cried one of these birds to him.

'Who are you?' screeched the other. 'You are a thief! Go away.'

'I beg your pardon, gentlemen,' the pickpocket replied. 'I thought you were just birds.'

Eventually this pickpocket was caught. In his defence he pleaded that he did not know that some men in Rani Nilmani's Estate changed themselves into parrots to bring trouble to poor vagrants with large families to support.

Though the ordinary green parrots are not as clever as the red-tailed parrakeets, they are certainly not stupid. They, too, might be taught to do a lot of things—from firing off a flintlock to telling fortunes by playing cards, from keeping an eye on a sleeping baby to driving away stray dogs....

But the main thing was to give those parrots in the mango-grove the necessary training. As there was no one to teach them anything they learnt simply to mimic the irritating cries of the peacocks and the equally disagreeable hootings of the monkeys, and to behave no better.

Fortunately, Mohan did not try to imitate the peacocks, or the monkeys, or the parrots. His natural intelligence and inborn grace probably saved him from being influenced by such unpleasant creatures as inhabited the mango-grove in their scores.

There is little to say about the timid gazelles and the wild goats. They could hardly be counted among the regular dwellers of the grove. They were so few.

Sister Svenska used to tell us that we children were apt to be influenced by those round about us. What a blessing Mohan was not affected by his neighbours in that semi-wild park.

My home was beyond the mango-grove. And each day I had to pass through it on my way to and from Sister Svenska's kindergarten. So I came to know a lot about the parrots, peacocks and the monkeys, and also about Mohan.

XXV

Mohan was frightened of me at first. He would run and hide himself in the tall undergrowth when he saw me passing through the grove. Sometimes he would run towards the remotest corners of the orchard, the most neglected and dark places where tall reeds and huge ferns grew.

By and by he came to accept me; that is to say, he did not mind my passing through the grove. He accepted me, I believe, as an unavoidable daily bother. Finally he ceased to be afraid of me. I never threw stones and sticks at him like those monkeys, neither did I try to peck at him like the peacocks.

Once I found him closely following me; the satchel on my back seemed to interest him greatly. I well remember that morning; as I passed by the Omkarnath temple I took my satchel off my back and removed my sandals to make my bow to the god of the temple in the usual way. When I stood up and turned round I noticed Mohan looking at me attentively.

Perhaps, without my knowing it, Mohan had watched me doing my *pranams*, bows made in prayer, for many a day, hiding himself in the undergrowth of the garden. Because on my way back from school the same day I found him bowing before the temple just as you or I would do.

'Mohan! You are a good elephant,' I cried. 'You are not like the peacocks and the monkeys who have no respect for anything.'

Believe me, Mohan did not run away this time. He seemed to have understood me. He was on his feet now and swung his trunk to give me his *salaams*. Perhaps he was trying to say 'Do you really think that I am a good elephant?'

Anyway, that afternoon he would not let me come too close to him. When I tried to stroke him he turned round and moved away a few steps.

'An elephant that bows before the temple all by itself,' I said to myself, 'must be a good elephant.' I had an orange in my satchel and I took it out and left it in the place where Mohan was paying his respects a few minutes earlier to the temple of Omkarnath.

I ran away home without turning back, and did not know whether the monkeys picked up the orange or Mohan got it.

Next morning, however, I found Mohan standing in front of the temple with the orange in his trunk. He was no longer afraid of me, and did not mind my coming near to him. Why had he not eaten the orange, I wondered? He had thought, no doubt, that the orange belonged to the satchel and ought to be in it. For I found him trying to put it back inside my satchel when I was making my bow to the temple.

'Mohan,' I said, 'Mohan, you are good and honest. This orange is, however, for you. I left it for you, and you should eat it. Don't you like oranges?'

You should have seen Mohan's eyes sparkle! He was delighted. No one had ever thought of offering him an orange. Perhaps he did not then know what an orange is, for he wanted to use it as a tennis ball.

I found him moving backwards a few steps and then throwing it to me! I caught the orange as it came near me and threw it back to him. He caught it cleverly in mid-air as though he had been trained to do so.... That was how Mohan and I began our 'orange-game.' From that day onwards we played with an orange every afternoon and then ate it, each getting half. Thus we became friends.

XXVI

When I called on Rani Vabani I found her talking to the *sandesh-wallah*, the pie-man.

This should have surprised a stranger, for she never took anything that was not home-made. But she was fond of trying out new things on others, and also of making herself sweetmeats, savouries and pies. When the *sandesh-wallah*, or the boy who sold *chanachoor*, fried nuts, or in fact any vendor of anything to eat, passed by her place, she was likely to stop him and have a long chat with him.

She wanted to know how they cooked their wares, and exactly how the batter was made and the nuts fried. Did they use milk or whey? Was mustard oil preferable to butter for that particular variety of savoury? Was red pepper better than green? She would ask many such questions, and then give the man a good tip and tell him to come back with new recipes. Whether she succeeded or not in getting all the secrets from these vendors I do not know.

I made my bow to her and told her, 'Rani-Ma, I am the boy who lives beyond your mango-grove. I have come here to pay my respects to you.'

'Ma' means, of course, 'Mother.' 'Rani-Ma' would mean, therefore, 'Rani, whom I consider to be as venerable as my own mother.'

'God bless you, Son,' she said, and turning towards the pie-man she asked him to give me a *pantooa*, a sweet pie. "Try it, my Son, and tell me if it is all right,' she told me.

I hesitated to eat the *pantooa*, but Rani Vabani did not notice my diffidence. She was engrossed in inspecting the different varieties of sweetmeats the pie-man had on his tray.

'But why the milk of buffaloes?' she asked him. 'Will not the milk of cows do?'

'Of course, Rani-Ma,' the pie-man replied. 'Only it is cheaper for me to use the milk of the buffaloes. The milk of the cows would do just as well, or perhaps better. As soon as your milk starts boiling in the pot, you pour in the juice of two lemons and start stirring briskly. And you take the pot off the oven and let the milk curdle nicely....'

'That's how I make my sweet cheese,' Rani-Ma interrupted.

'To make *pantooas* you need a fine cheese-cloth,' the pieman went on. 'You just squeeze out the water and then make a dough with your cheese by mixing it with some butter, the yolk of a couple of eggs, a pinch of salt, and some flour mixed in water. The dough should be kneaded well, and then cut up into small bits, each bit large enough to be rolled up into the shape of a duck's egg, and in the centre of each you put in a stoned boiled cherry....'

'Now, do you or do you not add some finely powdered cinnamon and cardamom to your dough?' Rani-Ma asked.

The pie-man made a long complaint about the rise in the price of spices, and especially of the good quality cardamom seeds. These were being sent abroad to give flavour to certain brands of toothpastes and what not!

I waited patiently with the *pantooa* on a tiny brass plate in front of me. I knew it was no use disturbing Rani Vabani when she was collecting information for a new variety of *pantooas*. She would, I was sure, try out the vendor's recipe and then make improvements on it.

The brass plate had nice engravings—of peacocks and laurels. It came from Jaipur, I could guess. Moradabad patterns were different.

A bluebottle settled on the top of the little white cap the vendor had on his head. It was an exceptionally fine specimen—almost like a bumble-bee. It started crawling along the top edge of the cap.... I wondered if Rani-Ma noticed it.... No, she was much too interested in the recipe of *pantooas* to bother about this bluebottle.

'In the centre of the boiled cherries,' the vendor continued, 'you may put in a large, transparent crystal of date sugar, replacing the stone. Or if you will, dried raisins which have been soaked overnight in a very thin syrup perfumed with rose water.'

'That's quite clear,' Rani-Ma said. 'But what about the brown crust?'

'For the coating,' the vendor drawled, speaking as slowly as ever, without taking the least notice of my impatience, 'for the coating, each piece of cheese dough, kneaded into the shape of a duck's egg, should be rolled into egg-yolk and then into finely ground breadcrumbs and powdered biscuits. The rest is simple. You fry your *pantooas* in a deep saucepan filled with boiling oil or *ghee*, clarified butter, or fat. Just a minute will do for each *pantooa*. As you take each one out, you drain off the fat and then put immediately your *pantooa* into a plate of sugar-crystals....'

'Each hot *pantooa* should be entirely covered up with sugar-crystals?' Rani-Ma asked.

'There you have it, Rani-Ma,' the vendor replied proudly with a *salaam*. 'This is my own recipe,' he added triumphantly. 'You won't get it from anybody else. But such *pantooas* are not for vegetarians.'

Just before he bobbed his head in salaaming, the bluebottle on his cap was joined by a gnat. 'Will these two have a fight?' I wondered. Both of these insects, however, flew off as the *sandesh-wallah* made his *salaam* to Rani Vabani.

'But you have not eaten your *pantooa*, my Son,' Rani-Ma said turning towards me. 'You don't like sweets?'

"Yes, Rani-Ma,' I said. 'I am fond of *pantooas*, but I would like to share this one with my friend. My playmate has not yet tasted such a dainty, and it would be a treat for him.'

'Who is this boy?' Rani Vabani wanted to know.

'He is not a boy, Rani-Ma,' I replied, somewhat embarrassed.

'He is not a boy! Are you then thinking of getting married soon? Who is this girl, then?' asked Rani-Ma.

I saw her wink at the pie-man, and both of them were smiling at me. My cheeks grew hot, and the veins in my forehead thumped. I must have blushed violently because Rani Vabani's expression changed at my discomfiture.

She took me in her arms and said:

'Now don't be so shy. My grandfather was betrothed at your age. And how old was I when I got engaged? Who is this girl? Is it Ayesha?'

'My playmate is an elephant,' I mumbled. 'He lives in your mango-grove, and plays with me every day. He is your tiny elephant....'

Rani Vabani seemed to be frightened at what I said.

'Little Son,' she gasped, 'my Little Son. You are not playing with Mohan, I hope. That strange creature will trample you to death when no one is about. Goodness! What have you been doing? The *mahout* told us that Mohan could never be trained, and you play with it every day!'

'Yes, Rani-Ma. I throw my orange to Mohan and he throws it back to me, and when we have played for a while we share the orange between us.'

'You surprise me! Is it true?'

'Rani-Ma! I came to ask you if I may become his brother? We have already become friends. I would love to have him as a brother.'

Rani Vabani seemed to be amused and surprised at my request. But she hesitated to give any definite answer.

'Could you please let me be at least a half-brother to Mohan?' I implored. 'He has been so nice to me. He chased away the monkeys when they wanted to steal my satchel.'

'Well I never,' stammered Rani Vabani. She seemed, by now, to be greatly impressed by what I told her.

'The *mahout* told me,' she repeated, 'that Mohan was a crazy elephant, and might go mad at any time. Now you say he plays with you. Mohan has then become normal?'

Then I told her more about my meeting with Mohan near the

Omkarnath temple and how we came to play with the orange. Finally my visit ended with my getting two baskets of *pantooas*, one basket for Mohan and one for myself.

Rani Vabani patted me on the head and said:

'Of course you may have Mohan as a brother or a half-brother, as you will. But the moment he shows the least sign of moodiness or craziness you must tell me. Then he will no longer be yours, and I shall look after him and send him to a *mahout* to get him locked up....'

XXVII

So Mohan and I became brothers and started growing up together, though it was I who did most of the growing.

I have already told you about the troubles which made Mohan more shy than other animals. His failure to grow up was, I believe, due partly to his excessive shyness and partly to his almost total isolation, and partly to his fear that he was not doing any worthwhile work. Let me now tell you how I came to think so.

When Madhukar Babaji's elephants were behaving like hogs and I found Mohan more depressed than ever, I thought I would ask our wheelwright for advice. (Peon-Dada was away on leave at the time.)

One day I found the wheelwright combing his beard; it was then dyed red with henna, and that was a good sign. It showed he had some time to spare for me.

I had a look at his huge cart-wheel dangling in the air, closed my eyes for a second and jumped right into his workshop.

'Little Son,' he said, 'it looks as though you have something heavy on your chest. What is it?'

'Cha-Cha, could you please tell me what one can do to make

Mohan grow? He remains almost as tiny as he was when he first came to Rani Vabani's house.'

The wheelwright smiled and tickled me under the chin.

'So you are worried about your brother? It is simple. Ask Rani Vabani to give him something to do. Something worth while and not too easy for an intelligent elephant. Something which will make him feel that he is not altogether useless. Idle hands toil for Satan, and an idle mind is the Devil's workshop.'

'But Rani Vabani thinks that Mohan is half-crazy, and that is why she does not give him a *mahout*. Mohan is getting no education.'

'He will get education enough in time. Only if you can make him feel that the sooner he grows up the better, then you will see the change. He loves you, and he will do anything to help you.' As an afterthought, the wheelwright added:

'Why not train Mohan to do some of the tricks of the circus elephants?'

Cha-Cha's remarks made me try to teach Mohan to swing a pole and carry loads with his trunk. He had not made much progress when something unexpected happened.

PART TWO

'The Greatest Evil'

I

A number of strange boys turned up in our locality. And it was not the season for mangoes.

I wondered what they wanted. Of course, even if the mangoes and the jack-fruits were ripe for collecting they had no business to be there. These did not belong to them, and they had no right to pick them. But with some people you never know! They think everything belongs to them.

When the circus came to the neighbourhood quite a lot of strange visitors would pass our way. Some of them would pick flowers, slash the stems of the banana plants, leave bits of waste paper all over the place, and then shamelessly try to carve their names on the bark of the old, old trees, planted long before the days of Job Charnock, founder of Calcutta.

'It is no use arguing with such people,' Peon-Dada would tell us. 'It is absolutely no use. You can't convince them. Can you argue with a crocodile or make a monkey change his ways? Reasoning will not affect such creatures. No use quarrelling with a hog. You may hit a hog on its snout but it will remain a hog all the same.'

'Can't we do anything for them?' I asked.

'I am afraid not,' Peon-Dada regretted. 'Remember Bhartrihari's saying:

A diamond you may draw
From an alligator's jaw;
You may cross the raging ocean like a pool;
A cobra you may wear
Like a blossom in your hair;
But you never can convince a stubborn fool.

You have to leave them alone. Keep clear of their path and pray for their souls. That's all that you or I can do. Even in the days of Rani Nilmani it was so. She was a wise woman, and made it a condition that no fun-fairs should ever be allowed on her Estate. These fairs, she suspected, would attract a lot of outsiders, and some of them would, no doubt, behave like monkeys, would pluck up her Persian rose-bushes, destroy her Chinese orange-groves, throw stones at her lovely gazelles, and make havoc of all that she loved so well.'

These strange boys had, however, turned up when there were neither fairs nor circuses in the neighbourhood. The Performing Pachyderms had disappeared some time ago.

What did they want?

It did not take us long to find that out. They were for pilfering what they could, and for spoiling what they could not steal. Over and above, they cursed those they robbed.

It was a bad business. We found them stealing birds' nests and breaking up the eggs of the swans and wild ducks in the nearby *jheels,* those expanses of water. They would not listen to us. When the grown-ups were about they would behave meekly, like lost lambs. But among us children they spread terror. They were bigger than the buffalo-boys, and, of course, much bigger than any of us at Svenska-Bibi's school.

One day they wanted to take away the trained monkey of the buffalo-boys and had a serious fight with them. They would, no doubt, have got what they wanted but for the buffaloes. The buffaloes came to the rescue of their drivers, charged the strange boys, and routed them without any difficulty. Angry buffaloes are as dangerous as wild rhinoceroses.

This lesson settled for good the attitude of the gang to the buffalo-boys.

In revenge they turned their attention on us and wanted to beat us up. 'Just for fun,' one of them told us.

Who were we? Just a handful. And they were many. We had a hard time. Bheem Sen's sling proved useless to drive these strange boys away. They took to the habit of throwing stones at us, and mocked us for going to school. Their stones proved much harder than Bheem Sen's walnuts and smooth pebbles.

Eventually, however, we devised a way of keeping away those ruffians.

~

Let me break off here to tell you that in those days we children had a peculiar code of honour. Who first framed this strange code and how it came to be handed down I have not the slightest idea. But the code, in brief, was simply this: Grown-ups must not be dragged into children's fights and quarrels, and other affairs.

If stung by a gnat or a mosquito we were entitled to complain, but if hit by a stone thrown by another child, however big, we were not to talk about it to any adult!

A mistaken sense of honour prevented our consulting Peon-Dada or Moti-Didi or Cha-Cha the wheelwright, or even Karin, about those much-dreaded boys who wanted us to join them and give up school altogether.

~

Most of the children at Svenska-Bibi's kindergarten lived in the direction of Moti-Didi's field. So we planned that in the afternoon those living in that part of Rani Nilmani's Estate would wait till Moti-Didi turned up to fetch Tommy Dum-Dum. Then a big procession would be formed with Moti-Didi at its head. Soetomo, Mazdoor, Bheem Sen, Heera, Ikramaudullah, Pooroosotyamadas, Seeta, Ram Chand and several others followed her in a long file. The strange boys were afraid of being caught by Moti-Didi and kept away from that group.

Tu Fan, Ayesha, Hari, Mammod, and a few others lived in the other direction. They would return home with the buffalo-boys as they went that way, too. This arrangement was brought about through Tu Fan's help. Of course we had to sacrifice our sweets to the buffalo-boys as the price of their company. The fear of the buffaloes kept the gang away from this group as well.

In the mornings we arranged to come to school earlier than usual. As these strange boys came from town, they could not arrive early enough to catch us. Moreover, in the mornings the paths and roads leading up to Our School were full of grown-ups going to work. It was the afternoons that mattered, and our grouping together to return home proved an extremely satisfactory arrangement.

Unfortunately, however, I could not be fitted into the scheme—because I was the only one who lived in an altogether different direction from the others, beyond the mango-grove, and no one else lived that way.

So the strange boys fixed their attention on me!

I was asked by the gang to join them and give up coming to the kindergarten. Most of them, I understood, stayed away from their own homes for days at a stretch. Some had run away for good! Some of them found fun in begging in the streets late at night and in picking pockets among the cinema crowds. At least that was what they told me. They told me, too, that I would be an asset to them because I looked so small and pathetic.

'Your long curls and thin face,' the leader of the gang accosted me, 'and those wide almond eyes would make many a fat woman weep and give us money.'

'We can dress him up as a little girl, too,' remarked another member of the gang, the boy with a flattened nose. 'As we have no girls among us he would be a real help.'

One of these boys generally smoked filthy-smelling *birees*, strong cigarettes rolled in dried leaves. He had signs of a moustache and beard, though he was not tall; but he was somewhat stocky, and had a heavy iron bracelet on his left arm. I instinctively took a greater dislike to him than to the rest of the gang. He tried to pull my hair. When I drew back my head he said: 'You don't know what fun it is to be a girl. I bet you don't. When I was a girl-friend to a strolling Snake-Charmer, I had a great time. I have seen the world.'

'That's why we call him Daku the Ex-Friend. He knows the ropes,' said the boy who always toyed with knuckledusters.

'Daku knows the ropes,' Master Flat-Nose interjected. 'The snake-charmer won't have him as a girl-friend any more because his whiskers grew too fast. Now Daku has learnt how to keep boys whiskerless.'

'You shut up,' shouted the leader of the gang. He was called Sardar, and was the biggest of the lot. 'You shut up!' Then turning towards me, Sardar said: 'And you, my curly-headed Pansy, you are coming to see what it is like to sleep with us in Hickey's Stables near Dharumtolla Street. Come along with us and find out what it is like.'

I told them that they would do well to leave me alone; and then I got my first sound beating from the members of the gang.

The next afternoon the same thing started all over again. This time, however, they were rougher...

And as days went on they became more and more cruel. Several of them would get hold of me and twist my legs and arms. Somehow they seemed to find great pleasure in trying to make me squirm.

Why did they want to see me cry? I refused to shed tears in their presence. This infuriated them all the more. Why did they vent their anger on me? Why did they call me Pansy? And use vulgar language and obscene gestures to humiliate me?

Was it because I was the smallest boy with the longest way to go? Was it because of my long curls? Was it because I had a thin oval face? Was it because I made a point of looking as neatly dressed as possible? Was it on account of my eyes? Were my eyes always stretched with fear?...

They wanted me to join their gang and disappear from the neighbourhood. They had noticed that I was friendly with Mohan, and thought they would succeed in inducing me to steal him from Rani Vabani.

Daku, the former friend of the Snake-Charmer, had told the gang that a pygmy elephant would be an asset to them. He had further suggested that Mohan could be blinded and mained and eventually trained to collect money for them with a begging bowl.

'It would be such a success in the *melas,* in the fairs—a begging elephant,' he had added. 'But without his playmate, the boy with the curls, the elephant won't stay with us. An elephant never forgets.'

'Even if Madho,' Master Knuckle-Dusters explained, 'succeeds in lassoing the beast and in blinding it, the wretched animal won't come with us, let alone stay with us unless we get hold of its playmate, the curly-headed boy. It would simply run away or starve itself to death. Daku the Ex-Friend is right: An elephant never forgets, just as a monkey never forgives.'

'Well, Pansy,' threatened Daku the Ex-Friend, pushing his heavy iron bracelet up his arm. 'Well, Pansy! To-day you will have to make up your mind. We want a plain answer. It is simply "Yes" or "No". It is no use arguing with us any more. Don't waste your breath telling us stories. No use whining that the elephant does not belong to you, but to Rani Vabani! And you have only been allowed to play with it! No more nonsense. No more arguing. I have been long enough with a snake-charmer to tell you that arguing does not help. It is just "Yes" or "No". Make your choice.'

'No,' I said. 'Ten times No. I won't beg for you, neither would Mohan.'

Strange to say, Peon-Dada's remarks came to my mind just then. I recalled his telling me: 'You can't argue with a crocodile! You can't reason with a hog! You have to leave them alone! You can't change the ways of a monkey!' I was willing to leave the crocodiles, the hogs, and the monkeys alone. But *they* were unwilling to leave *me* in peace.

'Weigh your words, you Mule,' growled Sardar, the leader of the gang. 'Think before you talk. If we can't get your elephant we will give you the beating of your life.'

'And Madho will get your Mohan all right,' Daku the Ex-Friend grinned. 'And blind it before we leave this place.'

'You won't hurt Mohan!' I cried. 'You won't hurt Mohan, and I won't come with you....'

I had not finished my sentence when a kick in my ribs and a sharp blow on my groin made me dizzy. I was attacked from all sides. I found myself helplessly sprawling on the ground. My *punjabi* was ripped from my back, my satchel torn away, my sandals pulled off. My arms and legs were twisted and my head was banged repeatedly against the pavement. Then several pairs of hands lifted me up bodily and used me as a battering ram against the thick wall of the mango-grove.

This time tears came to my eyes in spite of myself.

'Say when, you Mule,' I heard Sardar yap. 'Do you want me to insert the point of my knife in you where you would rather not have it?'

In my ears there came a buzzing sound as though thousands of angry hornets were round me, and my body felt as though stung by them.

'Yes or No?' Sardar shouted. 'Say "Yes" or we will kill you.'

'No,' I retorted feebly, and felt someone filling my mouth with dust.

II

It would be impossible for me to say how long my ordeal lasted. It might have been just a few seconds or it might have been a few minutes, or it might have been hours. When the suffering is intense it is almost impossible to judge how long it has lasted. Anyway, at that time it seemed to me that my ordeal was a prolonged one, and I endured it for an age! Even its memory is painful to me to this very day.

They would have gone on hitting my head against the garden wall, but an unhoped-for succour came in time.

One of the 'sentinels' of the gang espied a grown-up coming towards us. And at his signal I was dropped with a thud and the gang made off in various directions.

They were clever enough to install a few 'sentinels' whenever they were out mischief-making. They never tormented me when any grown-up was within sight. In the presence of adults they would quietly follow me or try to draw me into conversation.

But as soon as the long wall surrounding the mango-grove was reached they would start, as no grown-up ever came that way. The grove was really beyond Rani Nilmani's Estate, as I have already mentioned. Only those who wanted to pass through it would come by that road. Such people were rare. And this thoroughfare hardly saw any passers-by save Moti-Didi, Peon-Dada and myself.

Could a more convenient place be found for tormenting me? In that solitary spot any crime could be committed without detection.

It was therefore a miracle that the 'sentinels' reported the approach of a grown-up. And this unexpected eventuality saved me.

My body was bruised, my lips were bleeding, my mouth filled with blood, my whole frame was burning. My pain was heightened by the indignity the thugs were all the while trying to inflict on my sense of shame....

Yet in my ears, strange to say, vague snatches of music came floating from nowhere. Was someone singing faintly at a distance *Ohe Rosho Raj?* Or was my fancy playing me a cruel trick? How incongruous was this *kirtan* song at that time! Was a wandering

Vaishnava, a worshipper of Vishnu, really coming that way and beguiling his time with a song?

I waited with bated breath for a helping hand to lift me to my feet. But none came to my aid. And as the music in my ears slowly died away, I said to myself, 'A false alarm might have frightened away the thugs and I must make the most of this respite to get into the mango-grove before they return.'

I tried to stand but found that was impossible. I could not get to my feet. I managed, however, with difficulty, after a few unsuccessful attempts, to get on all fours and then to start crawling. It was painful beyond words. Nevertheless, I reasoned with myself, it was better to try to move into the mango-grove than to lie immobile on the ground waiting for an unexpected passer-by to offer me succour.

The reprieve from deliberate physical torture, brief though it was, gave me the necessary time to think and plan for my safety.

'I must act now,' I said to myself. 'I must get inside the mango-grove before the thugs discover their mistake.' I began crawling slowly. I wanted to hurry. But that was out of the question. My crushed limbs refused to hasten.

'Will they come back soon? Will they begin kicking me again? Or will they use their knife? Will they really change me into a girl and make me live in Hickey's Stables?' These were my thoughts as I dragged myself painfully towards the gate of the mango-grove.

This gate was not far from the spot where the thugs had dropped me. In spite of my tears which nearly blinded me, I could discern it. It might have been only a hundred yards away. Yet it seemed to my racked limbs so far, so very far, so very, very far....

'Shall I succeed in reaching the gate before they return?' I wondered.

'I must do my best,' I repeated to myself, 'otherwise what will Mohan do?'

But I could advance only at a snail's pace....

III

After their fight with the buffalo-boys, those young thugs tried to raid the mango-grove.

The plan was laid by that stocky fellow known to his companions as Daku the Ex-Friend. To own a trained monkey was his ambition. And as he could not secure the mascot of the buffalo-boys, he thought of capturing a baby-monkey from the mango-grove.

'Baby monkeys can be easily trained,' he had heard his Snake-Charmer say.

And the grove was the place to get not one but as many as he cared to catch!

'A forestful of monkeys,' Daku said to himself. 'What more do I need? I shall easily catch a few.'

But Daku soon discovered that even in a park packed with monkeys it was not easy to capture one. Monkeys are elusive. So he consulted his boon companion, Master Knuckle-Dusters, the boy who earned that name for his dexterity in wielding that weapon.

'There are scores and scores of monkeys and hundreds of peacocks,' Daku the Ex-Friend reported. 'And there is a temple in the grove. No one looks after it. What about getting Sardar to help us with a few "Commandos"?...'

He and Master Knuckle-Dusters made a pact and decided to help each other get Sardar's permission to organize a raiding party.

'These young monkeys and peachicks are so easy to train,' Daku casually remarked one day as Sardar was discussing when the gang should abandon Rani Nilmani's Estate for more novel adventures elsewhere.

'And we might get hold of that baby elephant,' Daku added, as he found his hint did not evoke any comment from Sardar. 'We could make up a nice party and give shows like the Snake-Charmer.'

'That would be great fun,' said Master Knuckle-Dusters.

'You ought to know all about training monkeys. Don't you? Didn't the Snake-Charmer give you some training?'

The remark of Master Knuckle-Dusters made Sardar chortle. And most of the younger thugs mistook it for a sign of approval, and they jumped to the idea: 'It would be so delightful to form a strolling circus.'

'A dozen trained monkeys, a dozen peacocks and a baby elephant would not be a bad beginning for a menagerie,' squawked Madho the Lasso. He was the hangman of the thugs, and was so called for his clever handling of hemp ropes, leather thongs and lassos.

Sardar was not eager to collect monkeys. He was, however, persuaded to sanction a small invasion party of 'Commandos.' His own interest in the enterprise was confined to rifling the temple of Omkarnath and giving some of his *chelas*, novices, a chance to handle house-breaking tools properly.

~

Daku the Ex-Friend and the 'Commandos' assumed that Madho the Lasso would easily succeed in roping a dozen baby monkeys and a similar number of peacocks and peachicks as well as Mohan. They would afterwards deal with the temple. Burgling an unattended temple in a secluded grove offered them no great thrill. But lassoing monkeys and peacocks was something new. It promised greater diversion.

These young thugs were town-bred, and did not understand the ways of animals. They did not know that to protect her kid even a tame goat will fight a pack of hungry wolves to the death, and if a baby monkey is lassoed scores or even hundreds of monkeys will immediately come to its help.

And this was precisely what happened when the 'Commandos' with Daku the Ex-Friend at their head made their descent on the mango-grove.

A fierce fight ensued between the raiders and the combined forces of monkeys and peacocks. The small band of thugs was taken by surprise. They found their weapons—the knuckle dusters, clasp knives, hammers, truncheons, lassos and house-breaking tools—were of little help in this unexpected combat.

Many of the junior 'Commandos' had their fingers bitten off and faces scratched, and some were dangerously mauled by the monkeys. Even a number of the veterans had a hard time. Madho lost the thumb of his right hand! Daku and Master Knuckle-Dusters had their eyes nearly pecked out by the incessant onslaughts of the peacocks.

The thugs had to beat a hasty retreat, and thought themselves lucky to escape with their lives. Instead of securing any booty they left behind them some of their most treasured possessions: a few clasp knives, some hemp lassos, a number of brass-knobbed truncheons, hammers, files, and a bag-load of house-breaking tools.

~

This disaster did not, however, prevent the thugs from making a series of further inroads with increased forces, to retrieve the precious objects abandoned in their unforeseen, inglorious defeat. Within a short time they became notorious among the dwellers of the mango-grove.

In self-defence these animals came to organize a sentinel system of their own. Whenever any members of the gang tried to penetrate into their sanctuary, either openly or on the sly, shrill alarm-cries would fill the air, and scores of monkeys and peacocks would fall fiercely upon the intruders. In defending their young, these animals remained as obstinate and as ferocious as ever. Not only that: in repulsing the intruders their counter-attacks became more and more relentless....

And the list of casualties among the thugs rose steadily.

When all attempts to recover their property proved useless the 'Commandos' had to admit total defeat. And the raiding campaigns were called off for good when Sardar the Boss had the lobe of his left ear clawed off by a 'king-monkey.'

By now Sardar the Boss had lost all interest in baby monkeys and peachicks. His missing ear did not seem to worry him much; he treated it as a minor sporting incident. But the loss of the bag of house-breaking tools made him more savage than ever.

And Daku the Ex-Friend had to bear the brunt of his anger. He was held responsible for all the casualties and the losses since he had first thought of the idea. He was thoroughly pummelled by Master Knuckle-Dusters at Sardar's command, and was asked to make honourable amends for the shameful rout in the mango-grove.

'Otherwise,' Sardar threatened, 'Madho will tie you up. And I'll try my knife on you. I'll do some surgery and change you into a baby monkey.'

To worm his way once again into Sardar's favour, Daku the Ex-Friend devised a new plan—kidnapping me and taking away Mohan as well. You have already heard something about the outcome of this scheme, and now you know why the thugs learnt to avoid the mango-grove. Let me now get back to my story.

IV

The mango-grove was my haven.

I had not known that I should not have been able to crawl all that distance to the gate. A hundred yards is not a long way. But it seems more than a hundred miles to a bruised and bleeding boy if he is not guided by hope. It was the fairy lantern of hope which led me to crawl on when everything seemed dark and my swollen eyes could hardly see, and the slightest shifting of position meant intolerable suffering.

I should have remained just where I was but for that. And I would have asked myself: 'What's the use of moving when they will catch me up any moment?'

And the gang would, no doubt, have returned as soon as they had discovered that the alarm was a false one. Or as soon as the unexpected passer-by had gone round the corner.... And they would have finished me.

Though each movement meant infinite agony, I found I was talking to myself as I slowly advanced. It was like whistling in the dark.

'Once I reach the mango-grove I shall be safe.... Once I am inside the gate they won't dare come in.... Just a few more yards and I shall be there....' These were the words I was whispering to myself to keep up my courage. And it needed all the courage in the world to move on when the least stir of my tortured body meant excruciating pain.

I was afraid my strength might fail me. I stopped for breath every few yards. I faltered more than once. I was almost overpowered by faintness. But I did not give in....

For all the while the thought of Mohan's safety was in my mind.

'Mohan must be warned,' I said to myself. 'If I do not reach the gate soon Mohan might come out for me.... I have never been so late in returning from school.... If Mohan comes out they will try to lasso him.... They must not catch him.... They must not blind my Mohan.... No.... I must reach the gate before they return.... What was that sound?.... Are they returning?.... I must hurry.... I must warn Mohan....'

And so I did succeed in crawling inside the gate. In how many minutes or in how many hours, I do not remember. But I reached my haven in time, before the thugs came back to look for me.

The struggle was worth while.

I was bleeding and almost exhausted. But once inside the grove, the feeling of safety gave me momentarily greater strength. And I easily managed to move some distance away from the entrance, maybe an additional hundred yards. I was now safely beyond the reach of a lasso.

Mohan had been waiting for me almost at the entrance to the grove. He must have seen my struggle with the gang. He quietly followed me as I crawled on inside. He was quite at a loss to see me on all fours.

'God be praised,' I said to myself. 'God be praised that Mohan is shy and never goes out of the mango-grove on his own. He wants Moti-Didi or me to take him out. But had they known that he was just inside the gate, they would probably have tried to lasso him. They would have dragged him out, and what would I have done then?'

~

Whenever a defective or a cracked gramophone record is played, I do not know why, but I am vividly reminded of those brief minutes I spent crawling through the gate of the mango-grove and discovering Mohan anxiously watching for me.

A cracked gramophone record goes on endlessly repeating the same words or the same few bars of music as though it contained nothing else. And my brain at that time must have behaved like such a record. One question only kept coming to my mind continuously. It reiterated itself endlessly without pause, without respite.

I had no answer to it. All the same, I was asking myself the same thing over and over again, as if the answer did not matter so much, as if the formulation of the problem were of greater importance than its solution. Or was the answer so dreadful that my mind refused to accept it? Was I, therefore, unable to conceive it?

'Had they lassoed and dragged Mohan out of the garden, what would I have done then?

~

'Mohan,' I whispered. My throat was dry. The dust they had put into my mouth had caked with the blood from my tongue and lacerated lips. I could hardly speak audibly. With difficulty I muttered:

'Mohan! Please help me to reach home. The thugs want to

blind you. They will kill me one of these days. Please don't let them put their lasso round you. Even if they get me, don't let them catch you.'

Mohan stood still and tried to put his trunk round me. He did not move, but suddenly started sniffing. Was it the smell of blood which troubled him?

'What are you sniffing at, Mohan?' I asked feebly. 'I have not got any orange for you to-day.'

And then I felt everything moving in a mad merry-go-round. There was a whirling sound. And all went black.

V

When I regained full consciousness I found myself lying in bed. Many days elapsed before I got enough strength to leave my bed and then return to school.

I was asked what had happened. But what could I say?

Our code of honour prevented my tale-bearing to the grown-ups. My silence convinced them that I had something to hide. They wondered if I had climbed a tree or had a fight with another boy. I was told:

'You have been taught a good lesson and that serves you right.'

I asked how Mohan was.

'He is all right,' they said.

But later on I heard that Mohan had hardly eaten anything during the period I was confined to bed. He had spent most of the time sighing and moaning outside my window, and had to be chased away more than once.

VI

On my way to school I met Mohan near the Omkarnath temple. He looked miserable and had a strange expression.

But he seemed very happy to see me on my feet again. He salaamed with his trunk, wriggled his ears to make me laugh, and then trumpeted with pride. He noticed that I had no satchel on my back, and had no orange for him. My foster-parents had decided that as a punishment for losing my satchel and my clothes there would be no more oranges for me till the end of the year. Mohan was very disappointed.

'Moti-Didi might give us some,' I tried to cheer him up, 'then we shall play as usual in the afternoon.'

This was the best I could do to give him some hope.

Mohan came right to the gate of the mango-grove to see me off. I noticed he had tears in his eyes. I did not like this at all.

'Tears of joy,' Peon-Dada once explained to me, 'they are all right; but tears of sorrow, never. They bode evil. Tears shed in sickness are permitted. Tears shed in repentance are necessary. But tears shed in apprehension of a calamity bode no good.'

Mohan's tears would have made me sad at any time. But at that particular moment, when I was going to part with him for the day, they made me sadder than ever. I recalled Peon-Dada's saying 'Such tears bode evil.'

'Am I then seeing Mohan for the last time?' I asked myself. 'I am so weak to-day. How shall I be able to fight those boys? They are bound to wait for me again at the end of school. And this time they will catch Mohan if he remains so downcast.' These thoughts made my own eyes wet, but I restrained myself. 'Mohan needs courage—even if something should happen to me, he must save himself.'

'Mohan,' I said, caressing fondly his trunk, 'Mohan! Be reasonable. Instead of eating and drinking and becoming strong and big, what have you been doing? Just starving for days? What good has that done to you or to me? This afternoon those boys will beat me up again. It will mean once again spending a long while in bed, if I manage to escape with my life. What will you do? Just go on shedding tears! We have always been good friends. Is this a friendly way to help me, by becoming thin and miserable? Won't you try to be strong? They are so many and I am all alone.'

Mohan did not let me finish all that I was going to tell him.

He suddenly started jumping as though he had been stung by a scorpion. Then he made a series of whirling movements as if he wanted to catch hold of his own tail.

It was strange to see him do this. It was equally strange to see him make a dash towards a distant part of the mango-grove and uproot a papaya tree and twirl it like a drum-major's stick. He threw it in the air and caught it again with his trunk before it touched the ground. And then he began once again to whirl around. 'Dervishes dance in that way when they become mad,' I was told once.

'Why is Mohan jumping about in that crazy way?' I wondered. 'Did he resent my remarks? Was this strange behaviour a sign of moodiness?'

Or did he want to show me that he had learnt the tricks of Pushkar Ram's Pachyderms during my sickness and convalescence? When I was trying to teach him a few of those tricks, on the advice of Cha-Cha the wheelwright, he had not been very keen about these lessons.

'Mohan, Mohan,' I called. But he would not listen to me.

As it was getting late I could not wait for him any longer, and walked out of the gate towards the school. My heart was heavy.

'Mohan—blinded by the thugs!'... 'Mohan—shut up for being moody, as Rani Vabani had proposed.... That would be terrible'.... 'There seems to be no other choice....' Such were my thoughts as I walked slowly on my way.

VII

I was glad to come across Peon-Dada near the Canal. 'So you have been playing monkey-tricks?' he asked. 'Now you look miserable. Did you have a good fight with your fellows? Or was it with the monkeys? Eh? Moti found you lying stark naked near the gate of the mango-grove and Mohan grunting over you. She wanted to know why you had not called for her pancakes. What happened?'

What was I to answer? I could not tell tales.

'Peon-Dada' I replied, 'did you not tell me that if I had nothing good to say it would be better not to say it?'

'Oh! Ho! Ho!' Peon-Dada laughed. 'So you are trying to shield someone. Well, as long as you do not screen someone who deserves the gallows, it's all right. Otherwise, it would be a monkey-trick.... And it is no good for a boy of your age to behave like a monkey....'

In spite of all that Peon-Dada had said about tears my eyes became wet. Peon-Dada noticed it.

'No tears, my Son,' he remarked. 'No tears. We must all take the rough with the smooth. The sooner we learn to face the experiences of life the better. Now you know the facts of life?'

Then, as though he were imparting a grave secret to me, he bent down and whispered in my ear:

'Only remember this, my Son. The game must be worth the candle. Monkeying is a game that is not worth much. That's all.'

'Peon-Dada,' I began.

'No apologies, my Son,' he interrupted. 'No excuses. I have not asked for any. And even if I did it is for you to retort "Have you never done anything foolish?" I tell you, my Son, there is not one in a million who can say he has never done anything foolish in his life. We have to pass through all stages as we grow up. There is nothing shameful in that. So why should you feel ashamed? Only don't hurt, and don't get hurt. That's all. I must make a move now. There are lots of letters for the folks over there.'

'But, Peon-Dada, I want to ask you something,' I implored.

And there must have been something in my voice which moved him greatly. His expression changed. He looked at me with tenderness and stretched out his hand to caress my curls.

'What is it, Son?' he asked gently. 'Do all elephants become moody?' I inquired. 'Well, you never can tell,' Peon-Dada replied evasively. 'If you asked me "Do all elephants die?" I would say: "Yes, most certainly. Just like men." If you ask me "Do all men become ill?" what shall I say in reply? There is no need for any man to fall ill. But, strangely enough, most men do. The same with elephants. Do all men become crazy? No. But all the same, some are crazy, some become crazy, and some others are half-crazy all their lives. Exactly the same with elephants. That's all.'

I found Peon-Dada's answer disappointing. 'What do they do with moody elephants?' I asked timidly, hoping Peon-Dada would assure me that Rani Vabani's remarks were made more in fun than in earnest.

'What do they do? Why, they are sent to a mahout and are just killed off. Mind you, elephants are costly, and no one would dream of slaughtering an elephant which is not really crazy. All the same, a dead elephant is not a dead loss.'

'How is it possible, Peon-Dada? What good can a dead elephant do?'

'You are telling me!' he said, and began fumbling about in his pocket. Finally he took out a whistle. 'A dead elephant,' he continued, 'is worth a sack of rupees. I mean *a lac of rupees.* One hundred thousand rupees. For the ivory. Ivory is costly, and is sold by weight, like gold. But now I must really hurry along. Look after yourself, Son.'

But in spite of his hurry he stood for a while looking at me musingly. Then he handed me the whistle! A whistle! My guardians never allowed me one. Did Peon-Dada know that?

'This is a present for you, Son,' he said. 'A present to express my joy at your recovery. Tradition demands that we should manifest our gladness when a dear one has escaped from a danger. And this is my way of showing my delight. I shall also light a lamp as I pray for you at the foot of my *tulsi* plant, the holy basil plant, when the Dog Star rises this evening. Don't blow the whistle in your home. It has a shrill blast and others may not like it. But you might train Mohan to come to you when it is blown. That would be fun.... So long, my Son!'

Thus I received the first whistle I had ever had. I was tempted to try it out immediately. But I thought, 'I shall blow it only for Mohan, and I may as well wait till I see him again.'

~

At Our School I gathered that the boys of the gang were behaving in the same disgraceful way as before. And there was no change in our arrangement about returning home in two groups, one under the protection of Moti-Didi and the other flanked by the buffaloes.

Svenska-Bibi, Karin, and all the others were happy to see me back. 'What is the matter with you, Little Darling?' Svenska-Bibi asked. 'You look pale. Come, tell me what I'm to do for you.' And Karin kissed me and wanted to probe into my mind. 'What is troubling you, my little dear?' She hugged me in her arms and passed her fingers tenderly through my curls, and I blushed without knowing why. Did she notice it?

Could they guess what was passing in my mind? Did they have any knowledge of the cruel humiliation inflicted on me by the thugs? Was I expected to share my problems with them?

'Squealing is not playing the game' or 'Squealing is not cricket,' if you will. How could I tell any grown-up about the thugs and about my worries? Though these were haunting me from the moment I came out of the mango-grove.

The day advanced and the shadows lengthened and my anxieties increased too. I was more concerned about Mohan than about my own self. I started musing, arguing and reasoning with myself.

'After all,' I thought, 'if the worst comes to the worst, I shall have to leave Svenska-Bibi's school and sleep in Hickey's Stables. But I need not pick any pockets. What about Mohan? Has he become moody? Will Rani Vabani send for the *mahout* and have him killed?... Will the thugs get hold of him and put out his eyes? What if I make a pact with Sardar the gang leader and tell him that I am willing to come with him and bring Mohan too?... Will they still insist on blinding Mohan?... They may do what they want with me, but they must not hurt Mohan. I would not mind being dressed up as a girl if they leave Mohan alone....'

'What would happen if Sardar breaks the pact? If, after I have joined him, he decides to blind Mohan?....'

It was a terrible thought. And without my knowing it I found my cheeks were wet with tears. I went out into the porch to dry my eyes so that no one could see that I was sobbing.

Once outside my tears dried up. What I saw made me shiver.

Mohan was scampering about the fields in the same mad fashion as Pushkar Ram's Pachyderms. At times he was trying to get hold of his own tail and at times he was attempting to walk on his hind legs like a circus horse.... And then he would suddenly lie down and roll on the ground as though he wanted to rub something off his back. Mohan with his four legs in the air was a curious sight. He seemed to have become completely crazy.

And what made things worse, some of the thugs were prowling about watching Mohan from a distance!

'As long as Mohan can be seen from the wheelwright's workshop or from the bookbinder's, there is no danger,' I said to myself. 'Not one of the gang would dare touch him in the presence of the grown-ups.'

I must confess I did not quite believe in what I was saying. I was trying to look on the bright side.

But what made silly Mohan leave the mango-grove?

Did Moti-Didi take him out to carry her laundry? But then she generally brought him back to the grove when the work was finished. Since the day the SAC put up those notices about elephants Mohan ceased to come to these fields without Moti-Didi. Even with me he had shown great reluctance to come near the Canal.

I felt sick, and told Svenska-Bibi that I was very unhappy.

'You are tired, my child,' she said, 'you are just tired. You had a bad shock. You need rest. Fresh air will do you good. Just go out and play for a while with Heera's goat or Mazdoor's donkey. You will feel all right soon.'

I went out again, but I did not play with the animals. I was too unhappy to play. I sat under a *neem* tree by the Canal, closed my eyes, and tried to think.

'Has Mohan really become crazy?' I mused. 'What Rani Vabani said will then come true, and he will be shot! Now I have no choice, I must accept the offer of the gang. Even if they break the pact they will not kill Mohan. They may put out his eyes.... But a blind Mohan is preferable to a dead Mohan.... Or do they know that a dead elephant is worth *a lac of rupees?*'

Nevertheless, my choice was made.

VIII

I found one of the boys of the gang sneaking into the shadow of the trees. It was the stocky fellow known as Daku the Ex-Friend.

'Hello, Curly-Head,' he greeted me. 'How are you feeling? Is it still "No"? We have a new cow-hide thong with us to-day.'

'It is "Yes."...'

'And Mohan?'

'I shall try to bring him with me.'

'That's a good *girlie*! Now you are talking turkey, talking sense! Eh? But it is no use *trying* to bring him! You will *have* to bring him.'

'Mohan has become crazy. He doesn't listen to my calls any longer.'

'Madho will see to it with his lasso. A blind Mohan will come to its senses in no time. He might be changed into a female elephant too.'

'So you want to blind and maim him?' I sobbed unashamedly.

'Unless you want us to kill him right away,' Daku replied in a nonchalant way. 'Do you think a crazy elephant with its eyes wide open will follow you about? Sardar, our Boss, already wanted to put out his eyes this afternoon but I calmed him. I told him to give you one more chance. Think it over and tell me "Yes" or "No".'

'Yes.'

'What a sensible little thing you have become, Pansy! We will wait for you when the school closes. Let the other kids go away. We shall dress you up as a girl where you got your last beating. A *ghagra,* a heavily pleated skirt, and a veil will do. As a girl your escape will be easy. The Boss will come in a *bokhra,* the veiled costume of Moslem women, and will be your mother.'

'Yes.'

'But don't come too early. The Boss thinks that dusk will be the best time for you and Mohan. Just fool around the school after four. We will keep an eye on you. No use trying to escape us. Understand?'

'Yes. I understand.'

Daku kissed his finger-tips and blew a kiss to me. I found that gesture revolting, and it was perhaps disgust that made me blush. He grinned at my discomfiture.

'You don't like kisses?' Daku sniggered. 'You need some teaching! Eh? Good-bye for the present, Pansy! You will be our *Chota-Bibi,* Little Miss, and so, I believe, I shall have to lick your tail and do kow-tow. But don't turn the Boss on me. I haven't done you any harm.'

He threw an orange at me and told me that it was for Mohan; then he disappeared.

I closed my eyes and tried to collect my thoughts. But what was there further to brood over? There was no way out.

IX

I must have fallen asleep. A grunt from Mohan made me start. But I was afraid to wake up to reality.

With my eyes shut, I tried to convince myself that it was all a dream—the events of the last few weeks, the presence of the strange boys of the gang, Mohan's moodiness, my impending departure from Rani Nilmani's Estate.

Was all this not just a dream?

Or a nightmare perhaps?

'Oh, if I could only be back in my village,' I thought, 'among the bamboos or under the tamarind tree! But who would take me there? And even if I could fly back on a magic carpet where should I find shelter? Where can an orphan lay his head?...'

'Why are those boys so cruel? What have I or Mohan done to them?' I asked myself.

A new grunt came from Mohan and I felt the orange left behind by Daku the Ex-Friend dropped on my lap. Mohan was trying to put his trunk round me in a friendly fashion. I opened my eyes and found him sitting on his haunches by my side. There was no craziness in his looks now. Or was I mistaken?

I patted him tenderly. Mohan snorted with delight.

'You have not become crazy, Mohan?' I asked, 'Have you?'

Mohan wriggled his ears as though to tell me, 'You make me laugh.'

'No, Mohan,' I said, 'this is no time for laughing....'

Then I poured out my heart to Mohan: told him all about the value of a dead elephant; how crazy elephants are shot; how the gang would take us away; how to make an escape easy I would be dressed up as a girl, and the leader of the gang, too, would dress himself up like a woman and pretend to be my mother; and finally I told him about Peon-Dada's whistle and about the lamp he would light that evening under his *tulsi* plant.

'Mohan!' I whispered. 'Peon-Dada says that when a prayer is made with sincerity, it is never made in vain. Oh, Mohan, don't you think that Peon-Dada's prayer this evening will help us? And now I shall blow the whistle Peon-Dada gave me to train you. But please don't touch that orange. It comes from the thugs—those nasty, cruel boys!'

Then I put my lips to the whistle and blew it—just for Mohan to hear. Its blast seemed to please him. He wriggled his ears to show his satisfaction. He seemed to understand me.

And now having unburdened my soul I felt much relieved.

The die was cast. There could be no retreat. There was no way out. 'Even if I allow my head to be battered against the garden wall, it would not change the course of events.'

X

What does a man think when he knows that within an hour's time he will die? Or be killed?

When I was staying at Chandernagore with my cousin I often visited a picture-framer's shop. And there I would climb on a cane seat which looked like an upturned fruit-basket. The seat was comfortable. But it was full of bugs! So often just after I had managed to scramble on it, I had to jump off hurriedly to avoid these vermin.

The picture-framer noticed my discomfiture one day. He dipped the cane seat in boiling water and killed the bugs.

'Little Son,' he said, adjusting the seat for me, 'sit on it now. It's all right.'

Then turning towards his assistants the picture-framer

remarked: 'I wonder what the bugs were thinking when I dipped the seat in boiling water and they knew for certain that they would die soon?'

'Bugs don't think,' I said. 'They don't think anything when you dip them in hot water.'

'Well answered, Little Son,' the frame-maker smiled. 'But I would like the Padre-Sahib to give me an answer. Padre-Sahib! What would a man think if he knew he would die soon, in an hour's time, say?'

The Padre-Sahib often came to the shop to get coloured prints framed. These were generally of men and women with crowns of thorns on their heads.

'It depends on the man,' the Padre-Sahib answered. 'It depends also on the life he has led. In a way, living is preparation for dying.'

The picture-framer was evidently not satisfied with this explanation, for a few days later I heard him ask the same question. This time he tackled the old schoolmaster who taught in the same 'College' as the Padre-Sahib.

The schoolmaster looked rather shabby; and his beard, grizzly and shaggy, did not improve his appearance. He seemed never to. have combed his hair in his life! But he was very particular about always carrying with him a small hookah. Naturally, he smelt of strong tobacco. The stench was simply awful. He was a kind man, all the same, and never made fun of me.

'I think I committed a sin,' the frame-maker told the schoolmaster, 'by killing so many bugs for the convenience of a single child. Is it right to extinguish so many lives for so slight a cause? Is it just to destroy what you cannot create? I wonder what the bugs were thinking when they knew their death was certain.'

'Do you assume,' the schoolmaster questioned, 'that the bugs are capable of thinking?'

'That was precisely what this child was saying,' the picture-framer replied, pointing to me. 'Our Little Son said that bugs don't think.'

'The child has answered well,' the schoolmaster remarked.

'What about the other questions?' the frame-maker asked. 'Was it right to kill so many for the sake of one? I am assuming for the sake of argument that the bugs would have killed the child but for my intervention.'

'The answer is equally clear,' affirmed the schoolmaster, as he began adjusting his hookah. 'Vermin cannot be placed on the same footing as men. You are a human being and the enemies of the human race are your enemies. He who puts vermin on the same level as men will reduce himself eventually to the status of vermin, and teach himself to be uncharitable to Man. God alone can show charity to all, and the mortal who claims to understand the ways of God is either mad or an agent of Satan who aspires to Godhood.'

'Are we then not to show charity to weaker creatures?' several voices were raised all at once, almost in a chorus.

'Show charity by all means,' the schoolmaster said slowly, and then after a few futile puffs to make his hookah work, added: 'But for Heaven's sake, use God-given common sense and your self-acquired general knowledge. Have you forgotten the story I told you some time ago?

'When Bramhadatta was King of Baranashi, that is to say of Benares, Dipankara Kassyapa preached in the Deer Park under a Nigrodha tree. His sermon was: Man must seek Truth and practise Charity. As the people were listening to him he noticed a hooded cobra emerge from its hole and approach the audience.

Turning to his companion by his side, the holy man enjoined, "Destroy that vermin."

'And his listeners discussed among themselves: "What sort of a man is this? He preaches charity and wants the destruction of a creature that has done him no harm!"

'"Destroy that vermin," the holy man insisted, "for the sake of charity. Man has been asked to bear witness to the Truth. And he who allows a fellow-man to be imperilled for the sake of a snake is a trickster of false arguments, a reasoner of half-truths, and a worshipper of *Mara*, the Demon of Darkness. Destroy the weeds in your garden otherwise the flowers will never bloom in it. He is a poor gardener who tends the weeds with the same care as his flowering plants."'

'I have answered your question,' the schoolmaster concluded. 'Bugs and snakes should be destroyed if they cross the path of Man. Be a Pratyeka Buddha, a redeemed man, yourself before you preach, profess or practise universal love.'

'Well answered,' remarked some of the assistants in the shop.

The picture-framer was, however, still unsatisfied. He noticed that the schoolmaster's hookah was not working.

'Perhaps the schoolmaster has no tobacco,' I thought. 'So much the better! I shall be spared that terrible stench.'

The frame-maker, however, did not read my thoughts! At his nod one of his assistants brought the big shop hookah. It was offered to the schoolmaster. And he began smoking with great satisfaction. The shop hookah did not, luckily for me, have the same foul smell as the schoolmaster's.

'Had those bugs been men,' the picture-framer began again, 'what would they have thought when they knew their last hour was at hand?'

'I know,' the schoolmaster replied, puffing away happily at the big hookah. 'I know there are men who are no better than bugs. They are guided by instinct in the same way as vermin. They live like vermin, they behave like vermin, and they perish like vermin. They never aspire to wisdom nor are they guided by reason. At their last hour they will behave like bugs and die like bugs, unthinkingly. Their way of dying may, however, make it seem that they are facing their end with courage. But as I have told you, men who live like bugs will die like bugs and will think nothing.'

'Well, Master,' several voices once more came at the same time, 'all men are not bugs! What do they think when they are on the point of dying?'

'Have you ever taken a walk before dawn?' the schoolmaster explained. 'Have you noticed how with the coming of the day various sounds fill the air? The song-birds sing and the choughs crow. They are all happy and they express their happiness in their own way. Catch a bird and blind it and see what will happen. In sorrow it will sing or crow, according to its nature. Try to smother a bird and notice again what sound it utters. A bulbul will coo and a crow will caw. What is innermost will come to the fore.

'But if you terrify the bird by trying to drown it before it is smothered to death, you will see that it will die without uttering the least sound. A panic-stricken creature will not sing. It will be in a state of stupor at the hour of its death....

'It is the same with men: Those like bulbuls will warble and those like choughs will caw, and those frightened out of their wits will fall into a coma and behave as though paralysed. The dazed will neither act nor think, but simply pass away.'

A newcomer joined the group as the schoolmaster spoke of the birds. He was much younger than the schoolmaster, and a very different sort of man altogether, though he, too, was a teacher. He was smartly dressed and clean-shaven. He never touched a hookah and did not smell of tobacco. They told me that he was a widely travelled man, and had crossed the *Kala-Pani,* the sombre waters of the Ocean. He held in profound contempt all the older people!

As a rule, this young teacher was rather rude in his ways. He contradicted almost everything uttered by his elders. Whether he was clever in his arguments I do not recall; but I do remember that he had a number of favourite ready remarks. For example: 'You can't talk of the Ocean to a well-frog, and an old man is worse than a well-frog.' 'India is the most backward country in the world because her old idiots refuse to make way for the young.' 'India's dead wood is smothering her young saplings.' 'Unless we do away with our time-worn ways we shall never progress.'

The young teacher's arrival was welcomed with winks and nods by those in the shop. Everyone looked forward to a heated discussion.

In other countries people pay money, I am told, to see men fight with their fists, and they are called prize-fighters. In some countries people find fun in watching dog-racing or cock-fights or bull-fights. In my part of the world people seem to take the greatest delight either in wrestling or in debates or arguments between persons of different views. To participate in a contest between two well-matched opponents is a privilege to be valued.

But it also causes much bitterness.

I have also heard that in the overseas countries there is lingering twilight which separates the day from the night, and between the sun and the shade there is penumbra which is neither the one nor the other. Mother Nature has given the inhabitants of those realms certain special gifts—the capacity for compromising, the art of grading, and the craft of adapting. It is not so with us. Our nights are suddenly shattered into day, and our sunsets bring in their wake immediate gloom, and we do not know what is penumbra. Nor do we know the blessings of moderation. To us a man is either a bringer of light and therefore a friend, or a messenger of darkness and naturally a foe. Thus, very often our debates degenerate into galling disputes, and the participants become lifelong enemies. Our nature abhors all compromise and half-measures.

So you may well guess why the shop assistants nudged and winked at each other and made signs to the young teacher as, he came in.

He, however, needed no encouragement to contradict the old man. He was ready for a wordy fray with anyone, and he hated a shaggy beard and matted hair more than anything.

'Won't you say something, Young Teacher?' the picture-framer suggested.

'How interesting,' the young teacher chuckled. 'How fascinating. I knew that our old schoolmaster was acquainted with a lot of things. But fancy his knowing the language of birds! Frankly, I must admit, the more I live the more I learn. Perhaps one day when I succeed in growing a beard as imposing as his, I too shall be talking about the bird-language. But that won't help anyone to understand the feelings of a doomed man in his last hour.'

"What would you say, Teacher?' asked the picture-framer, more anxious to get a new viewpoint than to encourage a debate just then.

'I was reading a French novel,' the young teacher intoned in a mock serious voice, 'and in it Cardinal Richelieu asked a soldier: "What would you do if you were told you would be dying soon?" The soldier did not say "I should sing a song or caw or mope." He simply replied: "I should begin writing for the benefit of posterity, a history of France." That's the spirit, I say. Instead of interesting ourselves in worthwhile tasks, we people of India have a mania for talking rubbish. We waste too much time in discussing nonsense. What is the use of bothering about the last hour?'

'Because the last act crowns the play,' the old schoolmaster retorted.

The young teacher had no ready repartee. But he was not the man to let anyone have the last word, least of all an old man. So he raised his eyebrows and puffed out his cheeks and made a noise in his throat.

This was, of course, terribly impolite of him, and all stared at him to see what he would do next....

'Well, old and learned one,' the young man spoke sarcastically, 'instead of talking about other people, let us have the benefit of your own hopes and fears in your last hour.'

'If I were in a state of coma I would naturally not be able to think,' the old man explained, somewhat upset at the turn of the discussion. 'Otherwise I would ask you to recall a song of Ramprasad which begins thus:

I know this Day will pass,
This Day will surely pass...'

'Can't you quote a modern writer, Venerable Master?' the young teacher interrupted. 'Why hark back to one long dead?'

'All right! I will give you something modern. Here is my answer—a poem which begins in the same way as Ram-prasad's song; it is by Rabindranath:

I know this Day will pass,
        This Day will pass....
That one day, some day,

The dim sun with tender smiling
        Will look in my face,
        Looking his last farewell.

Beside the way the flute will sound,
The kine will graze on the river-bank,
The children will play in the courtyards,
        The birds will sing on.
Yet this Day will pass,
        This Day will pass.

This is my prayer,
        My prayer to Thee:
That ere I go I may learn
Why the green Earth,
Lifting her eyes to the Sky,
        Called me to her;
Why the silence of the Night
Told me of the Stars,
Why the Day's glory
        Raised waves in my soul.
This is my prayer to Thee….'

~

What does a man think when he knows that within an hour he will be killed?

I was trying to find an answer for myself as I sat in the porch of Our School when the others had left.

'Are other people's sensations the same as mine? Do they feel in the same way as I do?' I wondered.

'Within an hour's time,' I mused, 'I shall be in a different world. Among rogues and vagabonds, cut-throats and thieves. I shall be counted among them. I shall become a stranger to Rani Nilmani's Estate. I shall be dead to the world I know and love.'

What was my feeling at that time?

It may sound unbelievable, nevertheless it is true: at that moment I experienced a sensation of relief! The uncertainty was over! There was nothing for me to do but to sit and wait till it became dark. And then I would move into a new world—the underworld of thugs and thieves.

Or was it no relief at all?

'Frighten the bulbul before smothering it,' said the venerable schoolmaster of Chandernagore. 'Frighten the poor chaffinch before drowning it. And you will find that the bird will not utter the least sound. A terrified man can neither sing nor think, but will fall into a stupor. He will be petrified. His brain will be like that of the paralysed.'

Maybe what I took to be relief was nothing more than a foretaste of this stupor—the emptiness of the utter agony of despair....

XI

'You are an Uzbeck!' someone whispered by my side.'An Uzbeck is said to be a most stupid creature. That's what you are!'

It was Daku the Ex-Friend again. He was leaning over me and fiddling with the iron bracelet on his left arm, as was his way of showing his impatience or dissatisfaction.

'I told you,' Daku continued in a subdued voice,'to fool about the school house till dusk. Did I ask you to sit here and mope? Sitting like a stone statue of Buddha in full view of everyone!

Aren't you an idiot? What would happen if any of the grown-ups asked you what you were doing here after four? If you squeal we will rip up your guts.'

'I won't squeal,' I stammered.

'Your moping will help us a lot! If a grown-up turns up he will think you have become moody like your elephant. You are an idiot, an Uzbeck. Go and play about till dusk. Call at the wheelwright's or at the betel-nut seller or at the bookbinder's. Don't sit here and mope.'

I got up. I must have sat there for a long time. My limbs felt stiff.

'Listen,' began Daku in a different tone. 'Listen! I want to ask you something. Something personal. Promise not to tell.'

I stared at him. He was now grinning, trying to be friendly, I thought, in his own way. He was loathsome, all the same.

'Do snakes grin?' 'Do crocodiles smile?' These thoughts flitted across my mind as I watched him.

'Listen, Son,' Daku went on. 'It is just between you and me and nobody else. Do you understand?'

I nodded.

'Suppose,' Daku mumbled in a low voice, a faint whisper, as he looked behind him to make sure that there was no one within hearing, 'suppose I spare you being made into a girl? What will you give me? How much money shall I get? Money, you know, makes a blind man see. Do you follow me?'

'I have no money with me,' I said. 'Where shall I find money?'

'Don't talk like a fool! I am not asking money from *you*. How much will your parents give me?'

'I have only foster-parents,' I replied.

"Don't waste time talking like an imbecile. How much will your foster-parents give me if I bring you back home safe and sound?'

'I don't know.'

'Don't know! What do you mean?' asked Daku. He seemed to be surprised.

Peon-Dada's remarks about money and the value of the rupee came into my mind: I did not know why.

'A rupee in those days would buy eight *maunds* of rice, several hundred pounds of rice,' Peon-Dada had said. So I thought one rupee ought to be enough to secure Daku if not several hundred pounds at least twenty pounds of rice; and that, I believed, was a vast amount, more than my worth.

'Tell me, Son,' Daku persisted, 'how much will your foster parents give me if I bring you back safe and sound?'

'Perhaps you will get a rupee.' This was all I could say.

'A rupee! You are kidding me, Son. A rupee for bringing you back to your people, who have horses and hounds and hawks and cars, and who live in a palace and entertain the *Lat-Sahib*, the Governor, and the *Jang-i-Lat*, the Commander-in-Chief!'

'I must tell you frankly,' I confessed, 'they may not give you anything, not even a rupee.'

'What? People who live in a palace, who have twenty doorkeepers! They may not give me anything if I bring their child back home! Are you not their child?'

'I am their child, all right. But I fear they may not give you any reward. But Moti-Didi might offer you a rupee.'

'Listen. Let us talk things over in this way. Suppose I bring you back home, safe and sound, will you give me your pocket-money every week? This is just between you and me. Understand?'

'I don't get any pocket money.'

'Lord! People who live in a palace don't give you any money? Why?' Daku was surprised.

'They are like that,' I made it clear to him.

Daku probably sensed that I was telling the truth…

'Well, Son,' he concluded, 'I can't help you in that case. I dare not take the risk. Just forget all about this talk. Only remember that Sardar expects you at dusk. He will be dressed in a black *bokhra*. He will be the Mamma. And there will be a few others in white *bokhra*. It will be a family party, and you will be just one girl among others…. Now don't mope. Just fool about for an hour or so.'

XII

I left the porch and decided to call on the bookbinder.

It was no use going to the wheelwright. He was bound to be busy in the afternoon, and would turn me out without any ceremony.

And the betel-nut seller did not like any of the children of Svenska-Bibi's kindergarten. They never patronized him, while the buffalo-boys did. So he came to the conclusion that we had some sinister motive for not buying his wares. We had no pocket-money, and even if we had we would not have spent it at his booth.

Moreover, I recalled vividly my first reception at the bookbinder's. It was a friendly one. We all liked the bookbinder. He was known as Daftry Cha-Cha to us children of Svenska-Bibi's kindergarten.

~

'When you grow up, Little Son,' Daftry Cha-Cha told me, 'you will have to give me all your books for binding. I shall engrave a special seal for you, a winged angel, and put it on the back of every volume.'

'Do you think, Cha-Cha,' I asked him, 'that I shall one day be so rich that I shall have many books for you to bind?'

'Of course,' Cha-Cha assured me, 'of course. Your fingertips already smell of the nice leather-bound books you will be handling, thousands of them! Just give me a hundred books every year and make me happy.'

'But where shall I get the money for books?' I asked.

'It is not a question of money,' Cha-Cha answered. 'It is not a question of wealth. It is how you are born, under what star. It is in the blood. It is in the bones, and in the very marrow of the bones. Some people are born that way; they will find means for securing their books because knowledge to them is more than food and drink. You will have your books all right, and nice books too.... And what will your people do with their wealth? They are wealthy, and you are their only child.... They are not going to disown you. And even if they do, you will get your ten thousand volumes all the same. Only don't forget your Daftry Cha-Cha when you grow up....'

~

Cha-Cha's remarks came to my mind just then. I felt I ought to call on him to pay my respects and to tell him, in silence, without uttering one audible syllable: 'Cha-Cha, here is the boy whom you praised and who promised to give you a hundred volumes to be bound every year! Here is the boy who raised hopes in you! Here is the boy who greatly appreciated your kindness and encouragement! He is now going to join a band of thugs, and will probably never handle a book again for the rest of his life.

Cha-Cha, will you forgive him for failing to fulfil his promise? Cha-Cha, will you miss him? Will you remember him?'

~

Our Daftry Cha-Cha came from Chittagong, and when I came to his shop I found he had a visitor from his native place.

This visitor was certainly a man of importance. He was seated cross-legged on a *charpoy*, the shop divan. And apart from Cha-Cha, all the others were on their feet.

'To show honour to a distinguished person,' Peon-Dada instructed us, 'you should not remain seated in his presence without his special permission.' So I guessed the visitor was of some consequence. Moreover, he was dressed in a way which made him conspicuous, in a yellow robe which looked like a *saree*. One of his arms was bare. His head was clean shaven. So was his face.

'Bless him, Sraman-Baba,' said Cha-Cha as soon as he saw me coming in. 'Give your blessings to this little boy. Let him be our glory as he grows up.'

I bowed at the feet of Sraman-Baba. He patted me on the head as he said: 'You would be a great man if you could be a good man; but this world has been difficult for you, my boy. Never mind. Be of good cheer and everything will be all right.'

Cha-Cha and others looked puzzled. This sort of formula for blessing a child came as a surprise to them. I presume they could not make out why I needed cheering up. Could Sraman-Baba read thoughts?

'You want me to give the boy the usual blessing?' Sraman-Baba smiled. 'So be it. May this boy achieve his goal and make all virtuous people happy. If he desires *well* he will attain the object of his desire.'

Sraman-Baba then continued the subject he was discussing before my arrival.

'There is nothing to prevent men,' he said, 'from becoming saints and angels, or demons and devils. What you want, you will have. Ask and it shall be given.'

'If that is so,' Daftry Cha-Cha interrupted, 'what, then, prevents every man from becoming an angel? I want to become a winged, heavenly being. How can I become one?'

'Do most men know how to desire *well*?' Sraman-Baba asked. 'Visit the *Jadooghar*, the Abode of Mystery, the Museum at Chowringhee, and there you will find a picture-parable in stone, a bas-relief, made some fifteen hundred years ago, and this will furnish an answer to my question as well as yours.

'The bas-relief shows a sage explaining the mystery: *What is the Greatest Evil in the Universe?* He is facing a dove, a raven, an antelope, and a crouching man, and not one of these knows how to desire *well*.

'"What is the greatest evil?" the sage asks, and the turtledove replies, "It is love! When I am mating, the falcon swoops upon me, and I am his easy prey. I am tormented with love, and love is my undoing. What shall I do to avoid the falcon? Tell me, O Sage, how can I satisfy my desire for love?"

'"What is the greatest evil?" the sage asks again, and the raven answers, "It is greed! I am greedy and when I am gorging myself I see nothing, and am then an easy prey of the fowler. My greed is my destruction, and at the same time it is my only joy. What shall I do to evade my untimely destruction? How shall I satisfy my insatiable hunger?"

'"What is the greatest evil?" the sage asks once more, and the antelope avows, "It is passion! I am passionate and blinded with rage and when I charge my antlers get entangled with the creepers or with the net of the huntsmen. I am caught like a feeble sparrow, the easiest of all preys. What shall I do to save myself? How shall I rid myself of my passion?"

'It is now the crouching man's turn,' I said to myself. 'Let me hear what he has to say. What is his problem...?'

I could not catch what the man said. Some of Cha-Cha's assistants quietly lifted me up and pushed me into a side room. They were all very strict about preserving our innocence.

'Everything in its season,' they would say. 'You must walk before you can run. Problems of grown-ups do not concern you, children.'

A few minutes elapsed before I was allowed to return.

Sraman-Baba was no longer discussing how men could become angels.

'That is a pity,' I mused within myself. 'It is a great pity. If only I could have wings like an angel! Then there would be no more bother about Sardar and his followers. Why does not Sraman-Baba repeat what a man should do to become an angel?'

I closed my eyes to offer a silent prayer: 'Lord! what prevents a man becoming an angel?'

'It is Fear,' a deep voice sounded close to my ears. 'It is your own failing.'

I looked up, startled. Was it said in answer to my unspoken appeal? It was uncanny. I was frightened....

"It is Fear,' Sraman-Baba spoke in a calm voice, a voice that carried conviction. 'It is the Great Fear that Mara, the Evil One, uses as his net to entangle mortals and bring about their own destruction. What is this ravenous greed? Is it anything else than an exaggerated fear of starvation? Does not this fear rob the greedy of his pleasure in food? What is this turtle-dove's love? This love that brings destruction? Is it anything else but the desire of possession, and the desire that is born out of the fear of losing. And this misgiving makes the joy of possession meaningless....'

Sraman-Baba discoursed on Fear and why one should avoid it.

'Have you never seen yogis and fakirs passing through fire unscathed? How do they do it? Have you ever heard of *Sadhus* and *Sannyasis* being attacked by wild animals? How do they manage to avoid the ferocious beasts? They are capable of achieving what seems impossible to the ordinary man because they are free from Fear.... Therefore, we should try to liberate ourselves from the bondage of unjustified Fear. Freedom from Fear is the *first step* towards happiness. There can be no happiness for the coward....'

He also recited some verses in Sanskrit: '*Satyam, Sivam, Sundaram*...' the meaning of which he explained:

'Neither Truth nor Goodness nor Beauty shall ever be attained by the faint-hearted.'

XIII

It was rather confusing, all these remarks and the discussions that followed. Nevertheless several thoughts stuck fast to my memory:

Fear is an evil which destroys.

A just man has no cause to harbour Fear.

If you are true to yourself, it is shameful to entertain Fear.

Your Fear will promote Fear in others, especially among those dear to you, even if they happen to be far away. And your courage will give them courage.

Unjustified Fear is a contagion which will infect the innocent and the unsuspecting. It will destroy you and those you love.

Have no Fear in combating evil. Evil triumphs only if Fear lets in evil.

~

Was it true what Cha-Cha told me a short while ago?

'Near Peshawar the Hindu King Puru was taken prisoner and El 'Hidr, vizier of the Two-Horned One, asked him: "Rajah Puru, how do you want to be treated?" And Puru replied, "Who are you to inquire such a thing of me? It is a question which only a king can ask a king." So El 'Hidr brought Puru before his master Iskander, the Two-Horned One, and said: "Here is a fearless man. He fought on all alone in the battlefield even when most of his followers had either fallen or fled. And when I asked him how should we treat him, he said he would give his answer only to a king." Iskander smiled and turning towards Puru said: "How do you want to be treated?" And Puru replied: "Like a king." Iskander's guards whispered: "Puru, are you not afraid of asking for such a treatment?" Puru replied as proudly as before: "No! I am a king, and no man can treat me in any other way—not even my captors." Iskander said: "You have spoken well, King Puru. I offer you my hand. You shall be treated as a king and as a brother, for you are a fearless monarch...."'

Cha-Cha remarked in concluding his story:

'Being a king himself, how could Iskander treat Puru in any other way?'

~

Both Puru, who was also called Porus, and Iskander, better known as Alexander, were born kings, and so they understood each other.

'But what is one to do if one is enticed into a snake-pit or captured by the devils? Will crocodiles and serpents treat you in the same way as Alexander did with Porus? Try to caress a crocodile and it will kill you. Try to kiss a serpent and it will bite you. If a snake asks you to embrace it, don't be tempted. If a shark begs you to love it, don't be beguiled.'

> Caress a rascal as you will
> He was and is a rascal still:
> All salves and sweating treatments fail
> To take the kink from doggy's tail.

'Destroy if you can the agents of Satan—otherwise they will destroy you. And after your destruction, they will return to bring about the destruction of your dear ones. No compromise with the devil's disciples.'

"Have no fear. A *Sannyasi*, a holy man, is not afraid of savage creatures.'

'Unjustified fear is a great evil. Avoid it.'

XIV

It was dusk when I reached the corner of the garden wall.

From a distance I could see a knot of people. There was a tall figure in a black *bokhra* as worn by some Moslem women. A number of others were in *sarees*, and a few boys as well. One had a bird-cage in his hand and the others had various baskets, pots and pans and pitchers.

No denying that Sardar and his gang were cleverly disguised! Had I not been informed beforehand by Daku, I would have taken them for a party of women, some Moslems and some

Hindus and their children returning from a *mela*, a local fair, or from marketing.

'I have told Sardar the Boss,' said Daku running up to me, 'that you have promised to be good. Here is a basket of oranges for you to carry. You may give Mohan some of these oranges.'

'Mohan won't touch your oranges,' I replied coolly, and kept on walking as though I were not in the least concerned with what Daku had told me.

'He won't! Has Mohan become as crazy as that?' Daku asked. There was surprise in his expression.

I did not answer him, and kept on walking at the same pace as before.

'A crazy elephant can be cured,' Daku remarked as he produced menacingly a large clasp knife. He felt its blade as though to inform me that it was sharp.

I could not help noticing his gesture, but pretended not to be affected by what he said.

'It is not difficult to make a crazy elephant tame,' Daku the Ex-Friend grunted. 'I know the trick. Madho will lasso it, and I'll do the job. And your Mohan will become as shy and as timid as a newly-bedded maid.'

'You won't touch Mohan,' I burst out and stamped my foot on the pavement. 'None of you will touch a hair of his head.'

'What's that?' bellowed Sardar, struggling out of his black *bokhra*. 'Did I hear you shout in my presence? I am the Boss here, and I give orders. Hey! You, Curly-Head! You are walking fast. Come and kiss your mother. Come on.... There is no point in trying to run away from your Mamma.... Hey? You want me to try my knife on you ... before I try it on your Mohan? I am the Boss, you know.'

'You are not going to touch a single hair of my head, and I

am not coming with you,' I said in a firm tone, the very firmest I could command.

And I kept on walking.

Now only Madho, Sardar and Daku were by my side, on my right. Most of the gang were left behind; they had not grasped that I was not going to join them but was walking straight towards the gate of the mango-grove.

On my left was the high wall of the grove, and from it the sound of the tread of many feet reached me. It seemed to me as though a number of people were walking within the grove, moving in the same direction and at the same pace as I was going. Only the thickness of the wall separated them from me.

'Who are these people?' I wondered. 'Who are those whom I cannot see but whose footfalls I can hear? Have they come to help me?'

'Hey! You have been talking too much,' yapped Master Flat-Nose. 'The Boss does not like arguing. You don't want us to try that knife on you? Do you?'

'Try, if you dare,' I said as coolly as before. I stopped walking and started undoing the buttons of my *punjabi*, leaning my back against the garden wall. 'Try, if you dare,' I repeated in a firm tone, and its effect was almost immediate on Daku the Ex-Friend.

'Eh? What is it, Pansy? What are you after?' Daku snivelled. He seemed to be taken aback by my attitude.

'Evil must be destroyed,' I spoke slowly. 'And I am not going to argue with snakes. You are all snakes and vipers, and all of you will be crushed.'

While undoing the buttons of my *punjabi*, I felt Peon-Dada's whistle tied to the chain of my *madoolee*, the charm which contained a tiny scroll of holy sayings. It hung round my neck. Like most young boys I wore my amulet in that way.

'Peon-Dada has told me,' I continued without faltering, 'not to argue with snakes and crocodiles. Nor to reason with scorpions and slugs. All that one can do is to destroy them. This is his whistle.'

I put the whistle to my lips automatically and began blowing it with all my force. Its blasts were ear-piercing. But I found this deafening shrillness pleasant. It made me feel somehow bold. I was not isolated now. I had the means to make my presence known even at a great distance. I was no longer cut off from the rest of the world!

The blast of my whistle woke up the whole mango-grove. Strident cries of peacocks and parrots and alarm-shrieks of monkeys filled the air. The silence of the evening was broken by an infinite variety of sounds as though in response to my appeal. Even the trees seemed to quiver and writhe and tremble in all their leaves....

You are never alone when there is a sound in the air even if the sound is as feeble as that of a dragon-fly on the wing or as vague as the cry of a soaring rain-bird hidden among the clouds.

Sardar's expression changed. His followers looked alarmed. Some of them started slinking away from the group....

'Have you squealed?' Sardar asked in a begging tone. 'Tell me. Have you squealed to that pig of a postman?'

'I'll slap your face,' I cried, 'if you dare call Peon-Dada names. I'll lick you and every one of your gang.'

All of them seemed to be cowed by my attitude. None of them had ever heard Sardar being told off!

'You are Evil,' I exclaimed, weighing each word like Sraman-Baba, fully aware of what I was saying. 'No mercy, no charity for Evil. You are doomed, all of you....'

XV

What caused the unexpected change in my demeanour that evening? Instead of trying to avoid the thugs and blushing at their filthy remarks and vulgar gestures, I stood firm.

Was it due to my determination not to compromise with Evil? They would kill Mohan, I feared, even if I accepted their terms. They would perhaps kill me too, I thought. There was nothing to be gained by compromise.

Was it the courage born out of despair? A stag at bay will die fighting a pack of hounds.

Was it the new faith instilled in me by the remarks of Sraman-Baba? You never can tell how much your mind takes in unconsciously.

Was it the blast of my whistle? It seemed to transmit a message.

Was it the shuffling sound of many feet walking over dead leaves, bracken, and branches on the other side of the garden wall?

Was it the alarm-call of the dwellers of the mango-grove?

Was it the prayer that was being offered on my behalf when the Dog Star shone and a lamp was lit at the foot of the holy basil plant?

What was it?

I do not know.

But I noticed that Sardar and Daku looked uneasily at each other while the straggling last remnants of the gang scampered hurriedly away. Master Flat-Nose nervously climbed up a tree by the roadside.

'What for?' I wondered.

'Look out, Sardar!' he shouted. 'Look out!'

Sardar did not pay much attention to that warning. He was glaring at me. There was anger mingled with fear in his look.

'You have squealed,' growled Sardar, gnashing his teeth. 'You have spued. And you will pay. Look at me, Pansy.'

'I am looking at you all right. Don't get excited,' I replied coolly.

I blew my whistle again. I was no longer afraid of Sardar in spite of his snarls. It was he who now seemed to be the more frightened of the two. Daku had taken to his heels a minute or two ago. So there were only the two of us, standing face to face.

'I am looking at you all right,' I repeated with emphasis. 'It is for you to look out.'

Yes, I was looking at him, straight into his eyes.

When the Sraman-Baba was discussing Fear, some agreed with him and some did not. But all of them admitted that yogis and fakirs are never attacked by wild animals.

'Gaze straight into the eyes of a tiger,' someone had explained, 'without fear and without blinking. And you will see how the tiger will try to avoid your gaze. Your first blink will decide your fate. If you blink before the tiger does you will be finished. The tiger will break your neck. But if the tiger blinks before you, he is done for. He will take your kicks lying down. Don't be afraid to look straight into the eyes of a tiger or of a *nil-gai* or of any other wild animal, and make it squirm.'

'Sardar, look out!' several voices shrieked from a distance.

'Stop howling, you pigs!' Sardar shouted back. He approached me with his knife drawn muttering all the while. 'I'll teach this swine. I'll finish with him....'

Sardar had no time to finish.

Whack! Whack! Swish! Swish! Whack! An uprooted papaya tree, straight as a mast of the barges on the Canal, knocked Sardar down. He rolled on the ground like a lifeless log.

Mohan was twirling this papaya tree with his trunk and was dragging behind him Madho the Lasso.

The lasso expert had succeeded in putting a rope round one of Mohan's legs and then had got entangled with his own weapon. The loss of his thumb had affected Madho's dexterity, and instead of his catching Mohan, it was Mohan who had caught him. Madho was now being trailed along the ground. His skin had been scraped off in patches from his back and limbs. His raw flesh was bleeding. He was yelling with pain.

Soon Mohan dropped his papaya tree and, encircling Sardar's neck with his trunk, began one of his whirling dances. It looked like a small merry-go-round—Madho being swept about the ground, the lasso that secured him tightly to Mohan shortening with each revolution—and Sardar suffering the same fate as his companion, held in the vice-like grip of Mohan's trunk.

It was a frightful spectacle....

Mohan had a few knife-thrusts on his flank. He too, was roaring. He was mad with rage.

A minute ago when in danger of my life at the hands of Sardar and his thugs, and when Mohan, too, was in similar danger, I was saying: 'Evil must be destroyed.' And now I had tears in my eyes for these agents of Evil—tears of pity for those who could not feel the least pity. Now I could not utter "No mercy, no charity for you, thugs.' My feelings were mixed—pity mingled with horror.

'Mohan,' I cried. 'Mohan! Please let them go. Don't drag them inside the grove. They will be torn to shreds by the monkeys....'

Mohan did not listen to me. He gave a wild grunt, and moved towards the gate of the grove, whirling as he advanced, whirling ... as though he would go on with his mad dance endlessly.

'The dervishes when they go mad dance endlessly,' I recalled.

'Mohan has become crazy. He has become completely crazy.' And I started running towards Moti-Didi's place.

'Moti-Didi will help me,' I said to myself. 'She won't say, like Peon-Dada, that Mohan must be killed. Mohan came to my rescue....'

XVI

What does a man think when he is acclaimed a hero? What would be his feelings if he knew that he did not deserve this honour? Maybe, he would be thoughtful and sad.

I don't know what others think or feel. But when they told me that I was like Badal, the Rajput boy warrior who held alone a company of the enemy at bay, I felt thoroughly ashamed. The more they praised me the more I felt humiliated. I wanted to hide myself in the mango-grove. But they would not let me leave my bed for some time.

'Because of the shock,' Peon-Dada told me.

I was now at Moti-Didi's cottage. It was much more comfortable than at my foster-parents' house. Here I was allowed visitors, and Peon-Dada was a regular caller. This privilege would have been impossible for me if I had been with my foster-parents.

I thought over this matter of being acclaimed a hero, and asked Peon-Dada's opinion.

'We have to bear,' he said, 'such burdens as fall to our lot.'

This was not very helpful. So I thought of asking Moti-Didi for her view on this subject.

~

Here I must tell you that though I liked Moti-Didi very much and she looked after me so tenderly, I had one prejudice against her.

What was this prejudice?

It was born out of a casual remark of hers. 'I will break this broom-stick over your Peon-Dada's head if he dares call me "A String of Pearls," she had told me when I gave her the news that for winning the fight against the SAC that should be her name in future. 'Instead of Moti,' I had reported to her, 'Peon-Dada says you should be called Moti-Mala.'

At that time I had argued within me that it was not fair that she should think of breaking her broom-stick over the head of Peon-Dada. 'There is nothing wrong,' I reasoned, 'in calling her Moti-Mala. Did she not save Mohan from being turned out of Rani Nilmani's Estate? Why should she not accept her well-merited honour? Does not a good deed deserve recognition?'

That prejudice was completely overcome when I in my turn came to be honoured as a hero. I realized, only then, how awkward it was to be praised.

"When you love someone, Son,' Cha-Cha told me long ago, 'you simply do all that you can to prove your love. And you ask for no reward. Your reward lies in making the object of your love happy, secure, and free from worry.

Moti-Didi did for Mohan the same as I did. I guessed she loved Mohan, and I, too, loved him. That was a close bond between us.

But during my stay at her cottage, I gradually made the discovery that she loved me more than Mohan, and her fight against the SAC was waged not to secure free firewood nor to keep Mohan in the neighbourhood, but simply to make me happy. She knew that I would be miserable without Mohan, and so she had decided, in the words of Cha-Cha, to do all she could for the object of her love.

~

I felt ashamed that at one time I had harboured prejudice against her. Anyway, as that feeling was by now gone, I felt no hesitation in asking her for her frank views about heroes and hero-worship.

'It is generally like this, Little Son,' she explained in her own way, 'simply like this: Everyone gives a little bit of help, and all these odd bits of help put together make a great achievement. But someone has to put the odd bits together. And he is called a hero. There is nothing wrong about it. There are heroes in every walk of life, and every day we come across heroes and saints. Heroes and saints know how to receive and how to give....'

Her remarks seemed to have no bearing on my problems. I thought she was not being any more helpful than Peon-Dada, so I had to put my question more pointedly.

'Moti-Didi,' I asked her bluntly, 'what have I done to merit praise? I have done nothing. I simply ran away from those people who wanted to cut me up with a knife, and then came to fall ill at your door. It was Mohan who did the fighting.'

'Well, Little Son,' she said, tickling me under the chin. 'It is like this:

'One day the Emperor of India, Jehangir, found a mouse rising and falling like a drunkard in the marbled courtyard of his palace. Like a drunkard it was running about not knowing where to go. The Emperor asked one of his *nautch-girls*: "Take the mouse by the tail and show it to one of the cats. Just throw it to a cat and see what happens." The cat was delighted; it jumped from its place and caught the mouse in its mouth, but immediately dropped it as though in great disgust. Very soon the cat showed signs of pain in its face, and the next day it was nearly dying. The Emperor said: "Give a few drops of opium solution to the cat." When the cat's mouth was opened they found its palate and tongue completely black. The opium lotion put the cat to sleep and after a few days it recovered. The Emperor asked: "Where is the *nautch-girl* who gave the mouse to the cat?" And he heard that she was sick and her palate and tongue appeared to be black. "Has she been given anything?" the Emperor inquired, and was told that she did not believe in medicine and would not take anything. Later on he was informed that she had died. They also told him that they had found many dead mice in the City of Delhi, and many men and women and children were dying in the same way as the *nautch-girl.*

'So the Emperor offered a reward to anyone who would tell him how to prevent the Black Death which was ravaging his beautiful capital. He called for his Vizier, his Commander-in-Chief, his Minister of Finance, and all the important men of his Court, and asked them if any of them would care to claim the reward. "No, Emperor," they said. "None of us can claim the reward, for the Black Death blows like the wind wherever it will and none can cage it. It stalks like an invisible assassin, and it cannot be shackled." And the Emperor doubled the reward because there were more victims of the Black Death.

'One day an aged official of Agra came to the Emperor's residence, and with him were a woman placed inside a large iron cage such as carry tigresses only, and a little child in a golden *howdah* on the back of an elephant. The aged man shook the Chain of Justice which was made of pure gold and was sixty cubits long. It carried sixty bells, and one of its ends was firmly attached to a battlement of the Emperor's residence and the other to a stone column on the bank of the Jumna. If any officer of the Emperor's Courts of Justice failed to redress a wrong, the injured person had the right to come to this chain and shake it and make the bells ring and thus give notice of his grievance and of his demand for an immediate hearing. This aged citizen prayed the Emperor to confirm without delay the judgment of his Law Court at Agra. He wanted an urgent decision on a grave issue.

"Let this woman," he demanded, "be impaled, and let this child be rewarded with a sack of gold mohurs."

"What have you done, woman?" asked the Emperor.

'"I have done nothing, Emperor," she replied. "I have done nothing to merit this punishment."

'"What have you done, young son?" asked the Emperor.

'"I have done nothing either, Emperor," he responded meekly. "I have done nothing to merit a reward."

'And the aged official of Agra said: "This is the woman that allowed the Black Death to pass through the gateway of your fair city of Agra, and this is the boy that has found the means of shackling the Black Death."

'"How is it so?" the Emperor wanted to know.

'"This woman saw a mouse running about in a strange fashion like a drunkard outside the city gate. Instead of destroying it, she said that the poor mouse was a helpless creature, and she would give it a drink in her house inside the city, and thus she brought it and the Black Death inside Agra. And this little boy has shown us how the infected mice should be trapped, and thus he has demonstrated the method of shackling the Black Death."

'"What have you to say in your favour, woman?" the Emperor demanded.

"'I did take the mouse—only out of charity. Charity is no sin."

"'Do you know, woman, if you shield an assassin out of charity you help assassination in general? Charity ill-placed is murder. You deserve the punishment that the law of the Empire has fixed for you and others like you, who through negligence help murder, assassination, and crime. Take her away!"

"'What have you to say, young son?" asked the Emperor. "A journeyman is worthy of his hire, and if he refuses his due reward he is deemed a fanatic, and a fanatic has no right to be at large; he is a breeder of revolt! Speak what you have to say, and as you are but a child we shall temper justice with charity."

"'The cage in which the mouse was caught," the boy replied, "was not made by me; the iron wires which fashioned the cage were not mine; nor did I prepare the bait which tempted the mouse inside the cage. It was only by accident that I had placed bait in the cage in which the mouse was caught, and put the cage in the sun and not in the shade. What reward do I merit? I am but a boy and I want to be treated as any other boy."

"'Has he spoken the truth?" asked the Emperor.

"'The boy has spoken the truth," the man of Agra said in reply, "but not the whole truth. We grey-haired men and others who are not grey-haired but in the prime of manhood and still others who are lusty youths, we all tried in vain to find a bait that would induce the mouse to come out of its hole and get into the cage. We set traps with tempting baits in a dark corner near the mouse-hole, hoping that would be the best means to lure it. But this boy took a piece of cheese as his bait and put the cage in a bright spot where we least expected the mouse to appear. He found the right method to trap the infected mice."

"'Citizen of Agra, you have spoken well," said the Emperor, and turning his gaze upon the boy, he added:

'"Have you heard, young son, what has been said? It is not the fashioner of the iron wires nor the maker of the cage nor the cows which gave the milk from which the piece of cheese was made whom we should reward. It is the boy who put the cheese in the cage and placed the cage in the right place who is worthy of our reward. The Black Death stalks like an invisible murderer by day and by night. You have shown us how this unseen assassin can be trapped. You are worthy of your hire. Accept the reward and depart in peace with our blessing."

'The boy accepted his due reward and departed....'

After a pause Moti-Didi said: 'Do you understand now, Son? You are the boy who placed the cheese in the cage and caught the mouse.'

'If anyone deserves credit,' I said to Moti-Didi, 'it is Mohan.'

'And what about my Little Son?' asked Moti-Didi as she patted my head and caressed my curls.

'Moti-Didi,' I said, 'as soon as I am allowed to get up, I will get rid of my curls.'

'Why, my Little Son? You know I love your curls, and you want to get rid of them.'

'You may like them, but some don't.'

'Who are those people, I should like to know?' said Moti-Didi.

'They wanted to dress me up as a girl on account of my curls.'

'Who are *they*?

XVII

For a long time a band of strolling criminals, consisting of a few young men in their twenties and a large number of young boys in their teens, had been causing an infinite amount of trouble to the Calcutta Police.

They had no fixed abode. They were interested in arson, murder, burglary and house-breaking, apparently for the mere fun of destruction. Very often it was noticed that they had committed murder without robbery. They slashed and maimed domestic animals, distributed drugged food and fruit among the unsuspecting, fired haystacks, broke dykes, damaged telephone and telegraph wires, kidnapped and mutilated children, and had, in fact, become a menace to all the villages in the neighbourhood of Calcutta. They were as bad as thugs in the days of Rani Nilmani.

High rewards had been offered for information leading to their apprehension, unfortunately without any result.

Therefore the police greatly valued the capture of Sardar the Boss, Madho the Lasso, Daku the Ex-Friend, Master Flat-Nose, Master Knuckle-Dusters, and of that section of the gang which were using the empty stables of a dilapidated house once inhabited by William Hickey.

The trial of the gang evoked interesting comments.

The newspaper reports were read out, I gathered, to an attentive audience every evening in the workshop of our wheelwright. And there were some serious discussions over the attitude of a number of spinster missionaries who were opposed to the gang being sentenced to long terms of hard labour.

XVIII

'I have no patience with these half-wits,' Moti-Didi declared one evening as she sat by my bedside. 'I have absolutely no patience with cranky spinsters. If they could they would all marry Sardar, the leader of the gang. Ask these women to choose between a mad dog and a sane one; they would go for the mad one! And this they call charity. My word! Charity indeed! If I could get hold of these cranks, I would break my broom-stick over their heads. If only the police could get some witnesses. Anyway, their thumb-prints on your bloodstained clothes proved useful....

'What is it, Son? What is on your mind?'

'Moti-Didi,' I whispered. 'Moti-Didi. If you only knew, you would hate me. You would hate me and not let me stay in your house any more. If you only knew....'

'If I knew what, Son?' Moti-Didi wanted to know. 'And even if I knew, do you think I would turn *you* out of my house? Now it is not Mohan who is crazy—it is my Little Son! I shall have to spend some money, I see. I shall have to buy some silken cords and a golden chain to tie up my Son. And that will cost a lot of money. And I am but a poor washerwoman....'

'Moti-Didi, I am not crazy. I am only telling you that if you knew that I am meaner than a worm you would turn me out of your house. I do not want to run away from *you*. I am much happier here with you than with my foster parents.... Don't cry, Moti-Didi, please don't. Only I am meaner than a worm.'

Then after a pause, afraid of the effect of my confession, I whispered softly:

'I am a squealer. Yes. I am a squealer. You may not believe it. But that is what I am.'

Moti-Didi burst out laughing. She leaned over me and rolled me over and over again, laughing all the while.

'Goodness! So I have a squealer as my Little Son!' she said. 'How strange! I thought you were going to tell me that you were the boy who tied Chinese crackers to the tails of Pushkar Ram's Performing Pachyderms.'

'No, Moti-Didi. I won't tell you an untruth. I did nothing to those pachyderms.'

'Sure? And you are not by any chance the boy who removed the wheelwright's spectacles and then put them back with thick blue paint on the glasses?'

'I never did such a thing, Moti-Didi. I did not even know until now that Cha-Cha ever missed his glasses and they were painted blue.'

'All right. I am glad to know that you never did anything with those ridiculous spectacles. But now tell me frankly. Are you the boy who drew pictures on the wet paint of the signal boxes near the level crossing?'

'You know well, Moti-Didi, not one of Svenska-Bibi's children would ever make such scrawls. Svenska-Bibi gives us enough to draw at her school. But what I did is much more serious. I squealed, and that is meaner than a worm.'

'Now tell me, Little Son. What is squealing, and what have you squealed?'

I then told her all about our code of honour, and how I ought not to have given away any details of my fight with the gang. At least that was very near squealing, I said. Could Moti-Didi keep me in her house after I had confessed such a failing?

'Svenska-Bibi would say "Nonsense! Sheer nonsense!"' Moti-Didi replied. 'And that is what I say now. Squealing indeed! If you see a nest of vipers, will you tell me about it or not? Will that be squealing? If you didn't utter a word about the nest of vipers I should be bitten to death, and so would Mohan. Squealing or no squealing, it is your duty to protect those that love you, and to protect them you must reveal the source of danger.'

Moti-Didi appeared to be very indignant.

'You take my breath away, Son. Suppose those boys,' she continued, 'had taken you away with the promise of treating your Mohan nicely and then had come back and taken away each one of the children of Svenska-Bibi, one at a time. What good would you have done by not telling us of the evil in time? ... Squealing indeed! Will you show me the man who first told you of this code of honour? I will break my broomstick over his head....'

It took Moti-Didi a few minutes to regain her breath. I had rarely seen her so upset. But as she regained her usual gentleness she took me on her lap and murmured:

'You have been reborn, my Little One, and I praise God for that. You will never lack courage to battle against an adverse fate. He that is reborn in fire shall not fade in the sun nor in the shade.'

XIX

A burden was indeed off my chest when I was assured that I had not squealed!

That night Moti-Didi heard all the details of our struggle with the thugs, and my confession ended with her adopting me as a Little Brother; and I adopted her as my Sister.

'At one time I had seven brothers and then I had none. Now I have one brother,' said Moti-Didi. 'Will this Little Brother order me about or shall I order him about? Anyway, I need not go to the jeweller to buy golden chains to tie him to his bedstead at night time. You are not Soetomo's tiger.'

'But Moti-Didi, you have not one brother but two. You are forgetting Mohan. Mohan is my brother. But if you do not want to have him as your full-brother, won't you have him as your half-brother?'

'That's right. I shall call on Rani Vabani and settle that affair. With the reward that the Police has offered you, and from what the SAC gave me some time ago, we may be able to buy him.'

'Now you go to sleep, my Little Brother, and I will sing to you.
'

From groves of spice,
O'er fields of rice,
Athwart the lotus-stream,
I bring for you,
Aglint with dew,
A little lovely dream.

Sweet, shut your eyes,
The wild fire-flies
Dance through the fairy *neem*;
From the poppy-bole
For you I stole

A little lovely dream.
Dear eyes, good night,
In golden light
The stars around you gleam;
On you I press
With soft caress
A little lovely dream.

From that evening onwards I never went to sleep without a song from Moti-Didi or a story. I was happy indeed. My only regret was that Mohan could not be by my bedside to listen to Moti-Didi.

Mohan was growing fast, and he could no longer get into Moti-Didi's kitchen for his pancake. It had to be served outside in the yard. Soetomo was lucky in this respect; his tiger did not grow up, and could be tied to his bedstead as usual.

PART THREE

In Quest Of Urvashi

I

'A grazing gazelle,' I heard from Moti-Didi, 'follows its own tongue and hardly knows where it goes. It skips over hedges and ditches without looking this way or that. Suddenly it lifts up its head and finds itself in a strange field. And it thinks it is lost.'

The same must have happened to me; for I skipped a few years without knowing, and found that I would soon be leaving Sister Svenska's kindergarten.

Christmas was fast approaching when I made that discovery.

To us as well as to others, Hindus, Moslems, Christians, Jews, Jains, Parsees, Buddhists, and even to those without any religion, to all who live in Bengal Christmas is known as the Great Day, *Barrho Din*.

We were very busy getting ready to celebrate the Great Day in our own way. This consisted of making toys and trifles to be given away to those we admired or cared for. Karin made us work hard.

What work did we carry out?

To be truthful, it seemed to me that we did nothing but play all the time we were with Svenska-Bibi. 'Work,' Peon-Dada told us, 'constitutes whatever you are forced to do. And play is what you do for your pleasure. If you find joy in your work, you are lucky. Your work then ceases to be work; it becomes just play.' If this be true then our work and play happened to be one and the same thing as long as we were at school.

Of course, occasionally we said to one another 'We are working hard.' But that was simply to repeat what we had heard from others, particularly from other children who did not belong to Our School.

In one respect, we children were like the *bandor-loks,* the apes. The monkeys of our neighbourhood could imitate very many things they saw men doing. Only they imitated all in a clumsy fashion, and had the knack of copying the more unpleasant actions of men. We came to hear of children being 'worked to death,' and therefore we were tempted to echo 'We, too, are working very hard.'

What work were we doing to greet the Great Day?

It was a secret well kept among us children. At least we thought we were working secretly, and Svenska-Bibi did not know what we were at. 'Svenska-Bibi, please close your eyes,' we would say. 'We are working in secret, and we do not want you to see what we are doing. It is a very great secret.'

"Is that so? But if I keep my eyes closed I shall fall asleep.'

'So long as you don't look at us, it is all right. We are working for the Great Day and you should not see what we are doing.'

'May I read or sew while you are working?' Svenska-Bibi would ask us.

"Of course you may. But you must not know what we are doing.'

Then within a couple of minutes, one of us would come to her and whisper: 'I have got stuck; could you please help me, Svenska-Bibi? So long as you don't know what the others are doing, it is all right.'

II

The Pandit from the *tol,* that is to say, the Sanskrit Seminary, had his hair arranged in a funny fashion. Of course I did not say a word about it to anyone.

Did not Peon-Dada advise us not to do anything unkind when there was no need to? Did he not counsel us not to smile or laugh at a man's appearance however strange it might be? Was he not right?

I had only to think of the reception that Mohan got when he was brought for the first time to Rani Vabani's side. Had not Mohan suffered enough for the laugh that greeted him, though it was not a malicious one?

'Judge not a man by his appearance, Son,' Peon-Dada advised me. 'Judge him by what he is. Judge him by his wisdom. Judge him by his ability to help and guide others. Only when you have gained enough experience of life will you be able to judge a man simply by his looks.'

When I first saw the Sraman-Baba he was dressed in a yellow *saree* which only a woman would wear. Surely many people would have found *that* funny. All the same, had it not been for his remarks about Fear I would have been in a different world to-day.

Thanks to Peon-Dada's guidance, an unusual appearance never made me laugh. On the contrary, it aroused my greater attention, and gave me food for thought.

So I must admit that the peculiar hair arrangement of the Pandit first made me curious, and then as I came to know him better I forgot all about the funniness of his hair-style.

What was this hair-style like? His head was clean-shaven but for a tuft of hair in the middle, and he wore that tuft long, made up into a knot, like Moti-Didi or Rani Vabani. This tuft was thicker than the pig-tails of some of the Chinese who were friends of Tu Fan's father.

The Pandit came from Puri, Juggernath in Orissa—the famous seat of Hindu pilgrimage and of Sanskrit learning.

He used to visit the bookbinder occasionally, and whenever he came there would be a cluster of attentive listeners round him in the shop.

It was from him I heard: 'Manna fell from heaven, but in the wilderness it tasted to each man like that sustenance he liked best....

'And the Voice went forth throughout the world, and each one heard it according to his capacity: the aged and the young, and children as well as babes. It was the same Voice that spoke, and each one interpreted it according to his own capacity of understanding. The Voice was to each one as each one had the power of receiving it....'

'Take for example,' Panditji explained, the roar of the Thunder.

'When the rumbling and the roar of the Thunder shook the Universe for the first time, it frightened the dwellers of the three worlds—the celestial one, the nether one, and the earthly one. They all asked the Thunderer: "What did the Thunder say?"

'And the Thunderer who made the Universe, the sky, the earth, and the nether world, replied: "What would you think the message to be?"

'And the angels who dwell above said: "Lord! Perhaps the Thunder trumpeted your message, and you speak in symbols. To us it seems that the Voice of the Thunder was: 'D—d—d—dd—.' Was it 'Doom'?"

'And the inhabitants of the nether world who are demons said: "Lord! Perhaps the Thunder gave your message, and you speak but in symbols. To us it seems that the Voice of the Thunder was: 'D—d—d—dd—.' Was it 'Doom'?"

'And the mortals who inhabit the earth said: "Lord! The Voice of the Thunder delivered your message, and you speak only in symbols. To us it seems that the Thunder said: 'D—d—d—dd—.' Was it 'Doom'?"

'And the Thunderer who created the Universe said: "If I speak in symbols then what would 'D—d—d—dd—' imply? And what would you do to avert Doom?"

'They all, without exception, answered: "To avert Doom, we must practise the virtue which has D as its first letter."

'And the Creator asked: "What is that Word?"

'The angels said: "*Daya,* that is to say, *Charity.* We should practise greater charity. Charity is a divine virtue."

'The demons said: "*Damanam,* that is to say, *Restraint.* We are passionate in our ways. We should exercise greater restraint. That would be the best means for us to practise virtue."

'The mortals said: "*Danam,* that is to say, *Piety.* We lack the spirit of worship. We should practise greater piety to acquire virtue."

'Then the Creator said: "To avert Doom, practise, therefore, those virtues."

'It was the same Voice that spoke throughout the world, and each heard it in his own way. But if each were to practise Charity, Restraint and Piety there would be no Doom....'

On another occasion Panditji from Puri said:

'Pramatha, whom the Yonas named Prometheus, was the Bringer of Fire and Kindler of Knowledge. He kneaded the earth with the brine and from this dough he fashioned Man. His dough was placed in different moulds. Therefore, men are as different as the moulds of Pramatha and those coming out of the same mould react in the same way even if they come from the ends of the earth. Men of the same mould hear the Voice in the same way....'

III

'Men of the same mould will not only hear the Voice in the same way, but interpret it rigidly in the same fashion.' That was what they said at the bookbinder's.

And I wondered if the parents of those who were at Sister Svenska's kindergarten came out of the same mould and therefore heard the Voice in the same fashion! Certainly we children were not of the same mould as our parents. About that we had not the least doubt.

Our parents came from all corners of the Indian Empire and from different parts of the world. Yet all of them had similar views on matters concerning us children.

Christmas was coming. The Great Day was approaching. Children all over the world were rejoicing. They were looking forward to their Christmas gifts. Those who did not receive toys would at least receive sweets, picture-books or other presents. We knew that was so.

But we had no right to receive presents. Our parents decreed it!

Sister Svenska could do nothing to change their views. No diplomacy, no cajolery, no arguments, no tears, could move these parents from their firm decision that their children must not receive any toys or presents.

Some pets were admitted, but not toys, Soetomo's tiger was tolerated because it was a tricycle which made possible his daily journeys to school. The sweets we received were from Sister

Svenska, and were to be taken with our meals. Not one of the children was allowed a book which had pictures. Such pictures as were in the text-books had to be covered up with daubs of Indian ink. The only picture-books we hungrily examined were at Sister Svenska's. At home we were not permitted to look at an illustrated paper.

~

On Christmas Eve, however, as a special treat, we were allowed to gaze at shop windows in the Chowringhee, and at Hogg Sahib's bazaar, and at Chadni Chak, and admire toys which we could not handle. We greatly appreciated this concession on the part of our parents.

We were generally chaperoned by one of the parents. A meeting place near Sister Svenska's was fixed. There the children would meet at the appointed time, and then they would be taken by tram to Chowringhee and allowed to inspect shop windows for an hour. If a child was a minute late there was no chance of his joining the party! He would have to wait another year for this thrill.

Though we never aspired to own any of the exhibits in the windows, yet we rejoiced in the mere fact that colourful toys existed, 'It is good to know,' we would say to each other, 'that there are such lovely things and that there are children who play with them in their own homes.'

Our speculations on Christmas Eve were different from those of other children.

With beating heart each child would pray that he might be permitted to join the group to be taken to Chowringhee.

There was no guarantee that at the last moment this

permission would not be withdrawn. We must not show too much jubilation or excitement at the approach of Christmas. Our parents had decreed that it was a bad thing to give outward signs of joy (or of sorrow!). Had they had the power, they would have controlled our inward manifestations of emotions as well. It was discreet to exhibit a certain degree of indifference to this journey to Chowringhee! Otherwise one ran the risk of being asked to give some help in the household at the very hour when all the children were expected to gather at the meeting place. A moderate show of indifference was prudent. An excess of it, on the other hand, was simply disastrous! The attitude would be commended but the child would be told that as he did not seem to be keen to go to Chowringhee it would be better for him to stay at home!

How could we show exactly the right amount of indifference? We children prayed that the Powers above would help us!

~

Those prevented from going out would eagerly await the return of the luckier ones for their report on the exhibits.

Was the window near the corner of the Grand Hotel more attractively dressed than the one next to the building of the *Statesman* and *Friend of India?* What about that tiny shop near the Corporation Mansions? Were there more trumpets this year? Any cheetahs? And what about the African animals, giraffes, zebras, and okapis? Was there a fat rhinoceros by any chance? A hundred such questions would be asked of the lucky visitors to the town.

The same question was in the heart of each child on Christmas Eve—would he be among those who were being taken to Chowringhee? Or would he be among the ill-fated ones? It was the uncertainty that troubled us most.

Those who were unlucky were not jealous of the others. 'Thank God! Mazdoor went this time. I was there last year so I must not grumble too much.' 'Anyway, Heera went and that is something.' That was the kind of thing we said.

~

It may seem laughable, but I must tell you that on Christmas Eve we all suffered from another apprehension.

What would happen if by any mistake a good angel or malicious demon brought a large toy car or a big doll for one of us? A tiny object we could hide. But if it happened to be a big one? What then?

Suppose Peon-Dada's temporary assistants at the Christmas season brought by mistake a gift parcel for one of us?

Had the distribution of parcels and picture-cards at Christmas time been in the sole charge of Peon-Dada we would not have worried. He would have done what was necessary to save us. But each year at that time so many new and temporary hands were engaged by the Post Office. It was extremely inconsiderate of the authorities, we thought, to engage strangers at Christmas time to help Peon-Dada! Peon-Dada might not have warned those new people that we were not allowed to receive any mail.

What would have happened, we speculated, if someone busily writing out addresses in a distant country had jotted down the address of one of us by mistake on a parcel, and this came to be delivered in due course in Rani Nilmani's Estate?

~

'There is such a thing as the Law of Probability,' once said the teacher of mathematics in the bookbinder's shop. 'If a million monkeys were put to the task of typewriting, they would, of course, type out a lot of nonsense. But if we gave them sufficient time, they would accidentally type out texts which would make sense. Give them an aeon, and sort out the papers, and you will find that without knowing it the monkeys have typed out all the books in the Imperial Library.'

'If this Law of the mathematics teacher,' we reasoned, 'showed that monkeys could accidentally type out hundreds of books, it was not at all improbable that some human beings could also unintentionally write out not one but a few addresses in Rani Nilmani's Estate. What would happen if Mazdoor or Bheem Sen or Soetomo got a parcel?'

How many days made up an aeon we did not know. But like that huge cart-wheel which dangled in mid-air in front of Cha-Cha's workshop this question, too, was a nightmare!

Would the parents forgive us for such an involuntary breach of the laws of good behaviour? Would they believe us if we swore that the parcel had arrived without our ever asking for it? Did they know anything about the Law of Probability which showed that the monkeys could, given sufficient time, type out text-books?

Even Peon-Dada, our highly-esteemed mentor, showed great deference to this teacher of mathematics. As a matter of fact, he had once lost a bet with this formidable pedagogue.

'At the Dockyard Post Office,' Peon-Dada had casually remarked, 'we sort out millions of letters. A million, maybe even a *crore*, which is ten million, I sort out myself at Christmas time.'

'That's impossible,' the mathematician remarked curtly.

'Why?' asked Peon-Dada, somewhat hurt at this brusque comment.

'Even if you had four arms like the elephant-headed Ganesha, the god of good luck,' the teacher taunted,'you wouldn't be able to count one million in a day let alone sorting out an equal number of letters.'

Peon-Dada, who knew all about the work in the Dockyard Post Office, felt insulted that his good faith and his speed in sorting out letters should be doubted.

'I work for eight hours a day, and sometimes for ten,' he declared,'and you will see with your own eyes how I can sort out a million letters in four hours. Let us fix a day. What about next Sunday? But bring me your million cards or envelopes.'

Peon-Dada made a bet. The teacher sniggered and produced two packs of playing cards from his pockets. He shuffled them automatically and put four aside....

'Why wait for next Sunday?' he asked Peon-Dada."Let us try it now and have done with it. Here are a hundred cards, as good as any postcards in your mail-bag. Just take them from the pack, one at a time, examine each card as though you were reading an address, and then let us see how quickly you can get rid of the hundred. The rest will be a simple multiplication....'

We all watched excitedly Peon-Dada counting the cards and the mathematics teacher looking at his watch and mumbling out the seconds and the minutes. To my great surprise and bitter disappointment, Peon-Dada lost his bet. He gave up the game in less than an hour!

'Even if you manage a hundred cards every minute,' the mathematics teacher triumphantly pointed out to all round him, 'and work for eight hours every day without a break, it would take you about twenty days to deal out a million cards.'

How he made his calculation I do not know. But Peon-Dada, Cha-Cha and others accepted his statement without demur, especially when they found that none of them could dispose of a hundred cards in one minute.

Such a man's remarks about the Law of Probability could not be lightly set aside!

~

Those of us who went out on the much-looked-for window-gazing expedition had our own way of examining the exhibits and of making comments.

Generally, our comments would be like this: 'Hallo, Ayesha! What do you think of that toy car? Not the tiny one, the big motor-car? The one which can take a small girl like you and two others. Is it nice? Did you say it was nice?' 'Well, nice in a way. But it won't do for me,' 'If the owner of the shop offered it to you, what would you do?' 'Thank him and refuse the present?...' 'I believe I would do the same, and tell him that it is not big enough for us....' 'We may be few here, but our family is big. Sister Svenska will not be able to get inside it, and what is the good of a car if you can't take Sister Svenska for a drive?'

At times one of us would say: 'This window is better arranged than the other. Bheem Sen ... Mazdoor.... Have a look. If we had been asked to put up that pile, we should have needed a ladder.' 'And even with a ladder it would not have been easy to take out one single toy from that pile.' 'The whole lot would tumble down.' 'It would be a pity to choose anything from that pile.' 'It would be a shame to disarrange it for one, especially as they look so nice now.'

A number of shops had jets of water coming out of a miniature fountain, and a ball held in the air by those jets. Such windows held our attention for many minutes. It was not enough to look at one such jet; the more we saw the greater was our thrill.

The party was taken back to Rani Nilmani's Estate before dusk. We did not get the chance of seeing the shop windows lit up. We were never allowed outside our homes after dark. Only on very rare occasions for unavoidable railway journeys, on the way to Howrah or to Sealdah, some of us had seen the blaze of the shop windows. Our parents thought it wicked to gaze at a brightly lit window. It was as bad as worshipping Sin Incarnate.

And these parents came from different sections of society; some were office-clerks, some artisans, some factory hands, some shopkeepers, some wheelbarrow men, and some very wealthy! They all thought alike about presents for children at Christmas time! They did not mind giving or receiving gifts where only adults were concerned. But, for us children, it was taboo to touch or receive gifts—whether at Christmas or at any other time.

IV

Our parents belonged to various religious denominations. Some were Hindus, some Moslems, some Christians, some Sikhs, some Parsees, some Jains, and some claimed that they had no religion at all.

The Hindu religion, just like the Christian, has its different denominations. There are Moslems who belong to different groups of Islam. It is needless to say that among the Buddhists, the Jains, and others, such, too, is the case.

And the parents of each one of the children attending Sister Svenska's kindergarten seemed to belong to a different religious group, rigidly separated from the theological persuasion of the others. They would seldom agree with one another on social and political issues. On problems of religion any agreement was impossible. On other questions, their opinions were equally at variance. They spoke different languages at home. Their tastes and standards of living had little in common.

Take, for instance, the child who came from Rani Vabani's palace. He came to Our School accompanied by a well-armed Gurkha, though he lived only a stone's throw from the kindergarten. It was the same with the children of the descendants of Tipoo Sultan of Seringapattam; they also came with armed guards. However, they came from a distance, from Tolleygunge. A number of other children also were brought to school by their *durwans,* men-servants or maids. They were all children of wealthy or well-to-do parents. And if I have not mentioned anything about them until now, it is because they were spared the trials which the rest of us went through at different times from the buffalo-boys and from the members of the gang of Sardar.

Had a stranger visited our parents and written a report about them, he would have said that there was nothing common to them save that their children went to Sister Svenska's kindergarten.

And how wrong and misleading such a report would have been!

This stranger would, no doubt, have told off Panditji as the young students did. He would probably have regarded the story about Pramatha as a mere Old Wives' Tale.

We children, however, knew that Panditji was right. We were absolutely convinced about it because we could verify it for ourselves from the behaviour of our parents.

'Those coming out of the same mould, into whom Pramatha breathed life, in certain matters think and act exactly in the same way, and they do not care to examine the cause of their peculiar behaviour,' so said Panditji. Our parents, however diverse might have been their ways, all held the same rigid views about the upbringing of their children.

Never was this fact made more apparent to us children than at times of festivity. Each Christmas reminded us to our sorrow that Pramatha, the Kindler of Knowledge, had put our parents into the same mould before he breathed life into them.

We did not mind so much being denied presents of toys and picture-books. We hardly noticed that all of us, the children of the rich as well as the children of the poor, had to dress in the roughest of clothes. We cared little that we were not allowed to get within a hundred yards of a cinema or of a lighted shop window. Neither were we worried about not receiving sweets or tasty food.

'What does it matter,' we would say among ourselves, 'what does it matter if we are not permitted to drink tea or coffee or chocolate or lemonade? But if only they would let us go to the Circus once!'

But our parents had declared that the Circus was taboo. And that mattered a lot.

~

At Christmas time several circus tents were pitched in the *Great Maidan*, the esplanade. Those were the big circuses. But a few smaller circuses paid their brief visit much nearer to us. Processions of trained animals and clowns with bands playing would pass through Rani Nilmani's Estate. Colourful handbills would be distributed. These told us something about what we would see if we were lucky enough to be allowed to peep into the circus tents.

Our desire to visit the circuses increased as Christmas approached.

Unashamedly we would stare for hours at posters announcing

their arrival. We knew by heart the number of lions, tigers, elephants, bears, zebras, giraffes, and other animals which were to be found in rival camps, and we would discuss their relative merits and demerits.

'What would we do if we were suddenly asked by our parents to choose the circus we preferred? Suppose they told us to make up our minds in a minute?'

Should Mumbo, the Pride of Africa, capable of playing on the horn and beating on the drum at the same time, be preferred to Jumbo the Great at Pagla's Parade Circus? The posters informed us that Jumbo the Great had a mathematical brain and could do multiplication.

'What about the zebras in the Accha Baboo's Company, the Unbeatable ABC?'

'But the ABC has not any Iceland Ponies fed on Iced Peonies. These ponies can dance through fiery hoops. And have you ever seen peonies?'

'Peonies must be like Muscat grapes.'

'I would like to see the performing seals in Maddo's Maddening Menagerie, the Unique M-M-M.'

As far as toys and shop-window exhibits were concerned, reports from others gave us consolation. But not so with the circuses.

It would have broken our hearts to hear any more details than those furnished by the posters and by the advertising processions which occasionally passed through Rani Nilmani's Estate. We were anxious to see things for ourselves, and at the same time we were afraid.

Were we envious of those very few who had visited the circus?

Who were those fortunate children?

Those who had their grandparents living with them; but not all of them. Just a few. Just a very few.

As a rule, our parents showed great deference to our grandparents, and readily acceded to their requests and whims, but only so long as they did not advocate anything for us children. On questions affecting us, none of our parents would make the slightest concession to a grandparent.

~

'They say swans never sing,' Panditji expounded. 'But sometimes they do, when they are floating on the Manasa Lake; and not always even there. The swans floating on the Manasa sing when they are dying or begetting their young ones. The Manasa Lake is not easy to reach. It is in the very heart of the Himalayas, and not many swans can fly over to it; and still fewer men will get the chance of being there to hear a swan sing. Therefore, for all practical purposes, it is quite logical to say: *Swans never sing....*'

'Similarly,' our Pandit explained on another occasion, 'they say ravens are black. But not all ravens are black. There are some white ones. But these white ravens cannot mix with the black ones because of their milky plumes. Neither can they mix with the doves, because they cannot coo. So the white ravens live apart, and they are so few they cannot form a flock. Thus they lead a solitary existence, a quality unknown among ravens. Are these white ravens entitled to be called ravens?... Taking all these various points into consideration, it would not be incorrect to say: *Ravens are black....*'

Nevertheless, swans sometimes sing, and all ravens are not black!

~

After nagging her son and her daughter-in-law for weeks, Seeta's grandmother lost her temper and threatened to leave the house if they still persisted in refusing her demand!

Grandma declared that she would go to Kalighat and sit on the steps of the temple with a begging bowl. She had been insulted enough!

'You have made me shed tears,' the old lady bitterly complained. 'I have been made to shed tears over a trifle. A child that receives no present is an unhappy child.... A girl that loves a pet learns what it is to shower affection on a weaker creature. Such a girl will become a better woman than one that has never had a pet.... Mind you, before I go to Kalighat I shall sit opposite the house and tell every passer-by: "The house opposite is the home of my son and of the woman who is his wife, and I am an old widow sitting here helplessly without a roof over my head—because they would not let my grand-daughter have a pet."

'I will not stay in this house a moment longer, and if you look at Seeta with glowering eyes, now or at any other time, because she wanted to accept my gift of a duck, I will lay my curse upon you before I leave the house.... I have been humiliated enough.'

Seeta's parents fell on their knees when they found the grandmother in that mood. Later on Seeta was asked to choose her duck, and she selected a tiny duckling in Hogg Sahib's Bazaar. That duckling gradually grew into a duck and came to be very fond of Seeta and the Grandma; but it would never approach Seeta's parents.

'Grandmother,' asked Seeta one day, 'I dare not ask for a present. But will my parents give you one?'

'Of course they will,' replied the grandmother.

'Do you think they will give you a brass ring, if you ask for one?'

'Surely. But why do you want me to have a brass ring?'

'Grandmother,' whispered Seeta. 'Will it be very wicked on my part if I were to ask you to lend me that brass ring so that I may put it round my duck's neck? There are some naughty boys who wanted to catch my duck, and when I told them it was mine they said: "What's the proof? It has no collar! How can you claim it to be yours?"'

'All right,' said the grandmother.

Later on the grandmother told Seeta's father: 'Get me two brass rings, wide enough to be placed round the neck of Seeta's duck—one plain brass ring and the other with tiny bells; and get the family jeweller to engrave inside the rings the date when I wanted to leave the house and sit on the steps of the temple at Kalighat with a begging bowl.... And get the brass rings before the sun sets.'

The parents did not say a word, but bought the rings.

That was how Seeta got her duck, and later the rings for it. But not everyone of us could claim to have such a grandmother!

And even such a grandmother could not get permission to let Seeta visit a circus. We knew, however, that the grandmother, through the intermediary of one of her nieces, had managed to let Seeta have a peep inside one of the circuses.

Did we consider Seeta lucky?

~

You may wonder how Bheem Sen managed to get his sling. He had no grandparents. But he had an uncle.

To make a long story short, Bheem's father owed some money to this uncle who had business connections at Moradabad, Jaipur and Delhi. Once he visited Calcutta and was invited by Bheem's parents to stay with them.

It was then Bheem saw this uncle for the first time, and discovered that he was a man of a very different mould from his parents. His uncle readily understood Bheem's longing for a sling.

'I have to buy some presents,' said Bheem's uncle one day. 'I would like to take Bheem with me to Hogg Sahib's Bazaar to choose them.'

Bheem's parents were struck dumb with horror. What a request! They tried to argue with Bheem's uncle about the undesirability of children handling toys, and about the virtue of educating the rising generation in Spartan ways, about godliness, and about other subjects too.

'Will you please try to get me a *tikka-gharee*, a cab, immediately, to take me to Howrah?' the uncle asked. 'I do not want to be under the same roof as those who have God at their beck and call. You seem to know such a lot about education—why do you not educate yourself to be polite to the man who lends you money without security? You refuse me Bheem's help. All right. Please get me a *gharee* and ask your God to help you with loans in future.'

That was the time when Bheem Sen's father was trying to make his store a paying concern. Hitherto it had been a losing one, and a source of great worry.

Bheem's father was a newcomer to Rani Nilmani's Estate, and for months his shop was little patronized. His neighbours were old-fashioned, and they hated the idea of trying out a new store.

Slowly, very slowly, he began to receive friendly calls at his shop. These visits were, however, not from buyers, but from neighbours who wanted to find out for themselves what sort of a man he was! Gradually, they started asking for old-fashioned brands, unobtainable elsewhere....

It took Bheem's father months to convince his visitors that he would not cheat them if they came to patronize his store.

This long waiting naturally meant losing money, and thus came the need to borrow. But who would lend him money? What bank would care to invest in a concern that was as good as dead? The Kabulis and the *Baniahs,* the moneylenders, would have asked for heavy rates of compound interest....

Thus the uncle came to be consulted, and an interest-free loan from him saved the situation.

Bheem's parents did not want the uncle to leave the house after a quarrel. They could not afford the luxury of estranging the person who had been their only support in their days of distress. They were quick to capitulate, for the uncle was known to be kind-hearted and God-fearing in spite of his occasional outbursts of bad humour.

'Of course, of course,' they said, 'if you are choosing presents for others, Bheem can accompany you. But he knows very little about presents. You want to buy toys. He does not care for such things, and we don't know if he would be much help. But if you think he might be, by all means take him with you....'

'You don't like to receive presents, Bheem?' the uncle asked as soon as he and Bheem were outside the house, 'You don't like presents?'

'Of course I do,' replied Bheem. 'But I am not allowed to have any.'

'What will they do if I give you a large mechanical spinning top?'

'They will thank you and wait till you are gone and then put it in the dustbin outside the house,' said Bheem truthfully. As an afterthought he added: 'They might burn it, too. The dustman might collect it from the bin and give it to his child, or someone else might pick it up. So I think they would put it in the oven, and when it was charred they would put it in the dustbin.'

'And what does your Svenska-Bibi say?' asked the uncle.

'She says nothing. She allows us to play all day long. There is a hobby-horse in the school. We can ride on it as long as we like. She just lets us play and paint and sing.'

'She says nothing?' The uncle was surprised. 'Then what does she do?'

"She plays with us. She sings with us. She...'

'She sings?' the uncle interrupted. 'And you are allowed to sing? What do your parents say to that? Do they know that you ride a hobby-horse at school?'

'Svenska-Bibi says that at school we are her children. At home we are our parents'. My father did call on her and asked her not to let me play with the hobby-horse nor learn to sing. She asked father why he had Moradabad brass bowls in our house, and father said that he came from Moradabad and he was at times homesick, and so she would understand. She said the big toy horse belonged to her. It came from Sweden, the country to which she owes a lot ... and he should understand....'

'Did he tell her not to teach you to sing?' the uncle wondered.

'Yes! He did. How do you know? He told her that she should not teach *me* any singing. He did not mind what other children did.'

'And what did Sister Svenska say to that?' the uncle wanted to know.

'Svenska-Bibi said that she praised the Lord at the break of day and at noon-day and at the close of the day, and as often as she could find time to do so. We children were welcome to join her in her songs of praise. Then she asked father if he was of the *Nihil-panthi*, of the Nihilist Sect, and father said that he was not.'

"Will you sing me one of Sister Svenska's songs?' asked the uncle.

Bheem Sen hesitated.

'Why don't you sing?' the uncle questioned. 'Does she teach you only *Kristani,* Christian, songs?'

'I don't know,' Bheem replied.

'Sing one of the songs. I won't tell your father. Just let me hear what sort of songs you sing.'

'We sing very many songs. It is difficult to sing without Karin. Karin sings first and then we join in.'

Bheem was afraid of singing. He did not know what his uncle really wanted! Then he was afraid that perhaps he had been a tell-tale. Telling tales, he knew, was bad. Had he told tales without knowing it as he answered his uncle's questions? It would be terrible, he thought, if he were taken away from Sister Svenska's school as a result.

His uncle patted his head and said: 'Don't be shy. Just let me hear one of the many songs you sing.'

Bheem Sen told us that his uncle's questionings made him feel uncomfortable; but the request for a song made him turn pale and then red. But as the uncle was insistent Bheem gave him a song.

> When I put you in the earth, Poppy-seed,
>   Poppy-seed
> I wonder are you cold. Are you lonely,
>   Do you need
> A little glow-worm spark
> Near your cradle in the dark
> Till you fall asleep and dream yourself a flower,
>   Poppy-seed?

When the dewy sunbeams call, Dragonfly,
Dragonfly
The bumble bees and humming birds, I wonder
Are you shy
In such a crowd to spread
Four wings of green and red
And go gathering golden honey from the lotus
Dragonfly?

When you reach the shining sky, Ababeel,
Ababeel
Do you touch the stars behind the clouds?
Do you feel
Brave enough to talk
With the eagle and the hawk
Tho' you are just a tiny singing bird Ababeel?

The few remaining days of the uncle's stay in Calcutta were all high holidays for Bheem.

At the end of the first day's shopping expedition both uncle and Bheem returned home empty-handed.

'Your Hogg Sahib's Bazaar is no better than the Chandni Chawk of Delhi,' the uncle complained to Bheem's father. I should say it is worse. I did not get a thing. Bheem was very helpful. Without him I believe they would have foisted a lot of junk upon me. I can't make out why your shopkeepers refuse to produce the things I want.... Anyway, it was difficult for me to make up my mind. You won't mind if I take Bheem out with me to-morrow?'

The parents could not very well say 'No.'

So Bheem went out again the next day and the following days.

As a reward for his services the uncle asked Bheem to choose anything he would like to have.

Bheem chose a sling. It was easy to hide it from his parents. It did not take up much room. His uncle agreed.

What service had he rendered to his uncle, we asked. Bheem told us that the uncle wanted a *full* list of everything that would make Bheem and his companions happy.

Bheem's original list was extremely modest. This surprised the uncle. Then his discreet method of questioning revealed that Bheem, like the rest of us, had been brought up with the idea that one should not reveal one's inmost desires!

'What about an ice-cream?' the uncle suggested, and gathered that though Bheem would not mind keeping him company, ice-cream was taboo.

'Why?' the uncle asked.

'Because it tastes nice and I like it,' replied Bheem.

'Then why on earth should you not have it?' the uncle inquired, somewhat puzzled.

'Because father says that if I start taking ice-cream I may grow to like it. I may even become so fond of it that I would miss it when it can't be had.... It is something like toddy, father says. If you drink toddy, you will grow to like it and you will drink more. Finally you will drink nothing but toddy, and find pleasure in nothing else. Thus toddy will ruin you,'

'Look here, Bheem,' said the uncle. 'I am much older than your father, and I have never heard of anybody being ruined by ice-creams.'

So Bheem had ice-creams with his uncle!

When Bheem told us this news we shivered! Our parents, too, had reasoned with us in the same way as Bheem's father.

'It is wicked. It is most sinful,' we had been told,'to eat ice-cream and to find pleasure in it. When you grow up you may do what you like. You may hang yourself, if it gives you pleasure. But so long as you are in this household you shall not get an ice-cream!'

I remember one day watching the ice-cream man selling cones to the children of the neighbourhood. His bell brought a lot of children out and they flocked round his tricycle. I watched how in a few minutes' time a large number were served and then the ice-man vanished round the corner sounding his bell. I had, of course, no money with me, and even if, by any miracle, someone had offered to buy me a cone, I could not possibly have accepted the offer. Ice-cream was taboo for me, so my foster-parents had declared....

But the mere fact that I had been near to the place where the ice-man had stopped his tricycle, and stayed on to watch a crowd of children show their ill-breeding by swallowing ice-cones, was enough to win me a severe reprimand. Later on I was caned. Not only that, I had to put on a conical cap commonly known as the Ass's Cap, and stand at attention for half-an-hour at the precise spot where the ice-man had sold his wares!

When his friends called on him, my foster-father referred to my tendencies as delinquency, and all of them expressed profound sorrow at my strange predilections. Some were, I am sure, genuinely shocked.

Was it surprising that we gasped when we heard that Bheem Sen had swallowed scores of ice-creams, iced drinks, cups of cocoa, tea, coffee, and other beverages with his uncle? Not only that, they had visited the Zoo, the Botanical Gardens at Sibpur, the Museum, the Temple of Parasnath, puppet-shows and cinemas, and even ridden on merry-go-rounds and swings!

Bheem Sen had asked his uncle more than once if he, Bheem, was not committing a grave sin by indulging in these orgies.

'Ask your Svenska-Bibi,' the uncle smilingly advised. 'She will be able to tell you if it is sin to enjoy yourself.'

Bheem Sen had not, of course, put this question to Svenska-Bibi because something happened shortly before his uncle's departure from Calcutta which frightened him out of his wits.

~

Sister Svenska seemed to be much moved as she read a letter. It was delivered to her at the same time as a huge sack.

'What is in that letter?' we all asked ourselves.

'Some of you boys have been talking,' Sister Svenska said as she eyed all of us rather severely.

From Karin we learned that the letter was unsigned. This heightened its mystery. Did it contain something nasty? Was it again one of those trickeries of the Sutasuti Advancement Company?

Sister Svenska took the boys aside and said: "So long as I can sew and knit and darn, I shall need nobody's money to run this school. Some of you boys have been talking to a stranger. How often have I told you that I am in need of nothing?'

Later on we came to know that the letter contained a large gift of money from 'an unknown admirer' of Sister Svenska, and the bag contained toys of all sorts from the writer of the letter. As he had no Swedish toys he requested Svenska-Bibi to accept those from Moradabad, Jaipur and Delhi. He had also sent a huge bell shaped like a lotus-bud. It sounded like a gong and was meant for Mohan!

~

Bheem Sen was very unhappy for a few days. He was frightened too.

He was afraid that he had broken the children's code of honour. Was he a tell-tale or a squealer? He did not know if in his many conversations with his uncle he had said anything which could be called tale-bearing.

He asked us for our opinions.

I passed on to him all that Moti-Didi had said about this 'squealing' business. 'It is not a code of honour, but a code of stupidity. This was what Moti-Didi told me.' I said.

'But,' some retorted, 'your case was different. It was a matter between thugs and you. With cut-throats there can be no code of honour.'

Finally, it was decided that Bheem Sen should confess to Sister Svenska, though most of us could not make out in which way Bheem Sen had broken any code of honour. But the fact that Sister Svenska's eyes were wet as she read his uncle's unsigned letter made Bheem Sen assume that his action must have been very wrong. It was not often that Svenska-Bibi shed tears.

So Bheem Sen told her all that had taken place between him and his uncle.

Sister Svenska's remarks about squealing fitted in very well with what I heard from Moti-Didi. We gathered that it was extremely silly to suffer for nobody's benefit and our idea about 'squealing' was all wrong.

'Bheem Sen has done nothing wrong,' she assured us. 'Only I did not know if he had solicited some money for me.'

'Have I done nothing wrong in drinking lemonade and in eating ices?' asked Bheem.

'No, my child,' Sister Svenska smiled.

'But I have not yet told you, Svenska-Bibi,' whispered Bheem, 'I have not yet told you that I have done something far worse.'

'What's that?'

'With my uncle I went twice to a circus,' confessed Bheem.

Svenska-Bibi laughed. 'That is no sin either. When your uncle comes back just re-visit the circus with him. Let us leave it at that.'

~

So, like Seeta, Bheem Sen, too, had been inside a circus!

Did we consider these two lucky? Did we envy the few others who, like them, had at one time or another been inside a circus tent?

Most emphatically not.

Instead of thinking them lucky, and envying their lot, we were, on the contrary, profoundly sorry for them. We pitied them from the very depths of our souls, for we trembled to think what would happen if by any chance their parents ever came to know that they had watched inside a circus tent clowns and jugglers and performing animals!

My foster-parents had warned me what would happen to me if I were ever found playing any indoor or outdoor games, handling marbles or tops, eating sweets, drinking tea or coffee or chocolate or lemonade, trying to visit the shows given by strolling players, riding a merry-go-round, blowing a trumpet, and, above all, going to a circus!

Once the children next door were being sent to a circus and their mother wanted to know if I would not like to join them. My foster-parents very politely refused the invitation on my behalf.

When she was gone, I was given a 'piece of their mind.'

'You must have behaved in a way,' they reasoned, 'that gave the good lady the impression that you would like to visit the circus. Now remember, once for all, that if at any time we detect in you the least desire to visit a circus, we will give you a thrashing and turn you out of the house.'

I nodded my head. What else could I do?

'Do you know Mr. Senapati from Siam?' they continued. 'Mr. Senapati, who lives opposite? He had a son of ten and a daughter of thirteen and no one else in this world. One day he heard that his children had visited a circus on the sly some five years ago. He asked them if it was true, and they admitted it was so. And what did he do? He branded them with a hot iron, and then stripped them naked and turned them out of the house. It was midnight. Next morning the neighbours found his daughter's corpse floating in a horse-pond and his son sitting in a tramway shed crying. The neighbours asked him to have pity on his only son and arrange for the daughter's funeral. Mr. Senapati said: "I have no son. Five years ago I lost my son and my daughter. I am not interested in the naked corpse in the horse-pond. Let the fish eat it.... The municipal scavengers or the crows will look after it."'

It must be admitted that my foster-parents were not inclined to be so harsh as Mr. Senapati!

'We won't turn you out at midnight, because you are as yet too small. But we will turn you out at mid-day, and we will let you wear a *langoti*, a loin-cloth, made of sacking. We are not as harsh as Mr. Senapati, and we won't brand you with a hot iron. We shall leave the punishment to the Lord, but we will put a garland of old shoes round your neck, and we will first give you a thorough beating.... So that your howls may bring all the neighbours to their windows, and your humiliation will be all the greater. That's what we will do, if you ever dream of visiting a circus.'

~

'The earth,' Panditji explained, 'is also *medinee* in Sanskrit because it contains the mead or rather the marrow of Titans who lived long ago. Titans were ruled by passion and not by reasoning. The detritus, or debris, of dead Titans, and the vomit of dead volcanoes, constitute each clod of clay. And Pramatha took a handful of clod and wetted it with brine, that is to say, salt tears—for the primal sea was not briny. Thus he made the dough from which men and women were moulded by his fingers. These were placed in the furnace of creation and life was breathed into them....

'As the Titans of yore were moved by passion and not by reason, men, too, at times manifest this primal desire to be swayed by passion. At times men show the tendency to revert to their primitive elements. But as each clod of clay was softened with brine, salt tears shed in compassion, those who have not been too hard-baked, show consideration for others' tears.'

Sitting on an upturned bucket in Moti-Didi's kitchen while she was ironing, I told her Panditji's story about Pramatha, and asked:

'Moti-Didi! Do you think Panditji is right? Do men of the same mould act in the same way?'

'I think so, Little Brother. But why do you ask this question?'

'If Panditji is right, then why was Mr. Senapati more harsh than my foster-parents? Mr. Senapati turned out his children from his house because they had been to a circus. But my foster-parents have now given me permission to go to a circus with you. Have they not?'

My question revealed a piece of news which Moti-Didi had up till now kept back from me, fearing it might hurt me and make me unhappy.

I came to know from her that my foster-parents had learnt that I used to play with Mohan on my way back from school, and therefore they would not have me any more in their home. I was at liberty to do what I pleased!

'My Little Brother!' Moti-Didi whispered, 'you who have lived all your life in palaces, how will you grow up in a cottage like this?'

I made it plain to her that even if my foster-parents changed their minds I would not like to go away from Moti-Didi unless I was turned out like Mr. Senapati's children ... and even then....

How did I succeed in abandoning my former dwelling place without a struggle? Because Moti-Didi's cottage gave me the feeling of being in a home, and that was a greater privilege than living in a palace. A gilded cage is not a nest. Nor every house a home.

From now on she was a real sister to me, and my guardian.

Moti-Didi told me that she had called on all the parents of the children at Svenska-Bibi's and she had pleaded for their permission to let the children visit the circus in the neighbourhood.

All of them had refused permission. Some had added: 'Rome was ruined on account of her circuses.'

Though Moti-Didi was anxious to take me to a circus, how could I go when this pleasure was denied to the others?

'And Tommy Dum-Dum's father?' I asked. 'What did he say?'

'Oh, he was different,' replied Moti-Didi. 'He was very different from the others. He said he did not mind if someone would care to look after Tommy. He himself is too busy; he is trying to rent a hall, and he can't find one.'

'He wants to rent a hall?' I was surprised.

'Yes. He wants to rent a big room for one day, so that he can pray there with other men of his country. It is a special occasion, the eve of the Great Day, and Tommy Dum-Dum's father would like to have a hall where no one would disturb the worshippers.'

'But Moti-Didi,' I asked, 'can he not pray in a temple or in a mosque or in a church?'

'Little Brother, God will hear our prayer wherever we offer it with sincerity. Only sometimes it is necessary to worship with others to gain greater strength for our devotion. And it is well that Tommy Dum-Dum's father should on Christmas Eve meet his own people to pray.... But he cannot find a hall because he and his fellows belong to a different Christian faith. They call themselves Exiles.'

'They can't go to any of the churches here and worship in their own way?'

'No, my Little Brother,' said Moti-Didi. 'They can't. Because their ways are different. It is like this, my Little One: If you go to Kalighat you worship by sacrificing a goat. If you go to the Omkarnath temple you are not allowed to sacrifice any animal, you offer flowers and fruits. If you are a Yihudi and go to a synagogue you put on a Yihudi headgear.... And God does not mind in which way you worship him so long as you do not abuse his Creation. But men are not angels....

'There was a man of God called Ibrahim,' Moti-Didi went on. 'He was famed for his holiness. Once at nightfall an old man knocked at Ibrahim's door and prayed for food and shelter. And Ibrahim saw that the old man was a stranger who had lost his way. Moved by pity he took the old man in and put food and drink before him. The wayfarer broke bread and thanked Ibrahim for his kindness.

'"Old father," Ibrahim asked, "why do you not thank God before taking your meal?"

'And the old traveller said that he worshipped the Sun only, and as it was dark there was no need for him to offer thanks to the Sun. This made Ibrahim very angry, and he turned the visitor out of his house.

'But in the middle of the night a voice rebuked Ibrahim.

'"Ibrahim! Ibrahim!" it cried. "Why did you turn the stranger out? God has borne with him for more than four score years. Could you not bear with him for one night? Are you more just than God?" And Ibrahim wept. He repented....

'And mind you, my Little Brother, most men are not like Ibrahim. They are far more severe. Some men worship God in one way and some in another, and each man thinks his own way is the best. That's the trouble. That is why no one wants to help Tommy's father.'

'Cannot Tommy Dum-Dum's father talk to Svenska-Bibi?' I asked. 'I am sure she will let him use Our School for his prayer meeting.'

'That's a good idea!' Moti-Didi remarked. 'God will bless you, Little Brother.'

She seemed to have something on her mind. There was a pause. Whenever she had something important to tell me there was such a period of uneasy silence. She wanted me to follow her remarks attentively.

'We must be nice to all people,' Moti-Didi said finally, 'but especially to strangers because they are far from their own people. And it is hard to be away from home and never hear one's mother-tongue.

'A dire punishment was meted out to some people living near *Kanya Koomaree*, the Cape Virgin Maiden, better known as Cape Comorin, because they were uncharitable to a stranger who sought hospitality in their midst.

'A stranger from the north was on a pilgrimage to Kandy, where a tooth of Buddha is preserved. Near Kanya Koomaree, Cape Comorin, he begged for rest and refreshment in a village. But the villagers offered him no help. Not only that, they set their dogs on him!

'"Why are you unkind to me?" the pilgrim asked. "I have done you no harm."

'"You haven't," the villagers jeered. "But we don't like strangers. You wear strange clothes and have a strange accent...."

'"I am a stranger," he replied. "I cannot help being different from you. Wouldn't *your* clothes and *your* accent appear equally strange if you were in my country?"

'"Certainly not!" they sneered. "And you bet we will never set foot in your part of the world even if it be the earthly paradise. God Almighty will not induce us to travel north."

'"Now, listen," said the pilgrim from the north. "Do what you will, but do not take the name of God in vain. It's no good blaspheming."

'"Ho! Ho! Ho! You are a holy one!" the villagers roared. "You seem to be an insolent fellow, you Kashmiri! Or are you a Sindhi? Or a Baluchi? Get out of our sight, or we'll break your bones."

'They drove the poor man away from the shade of the banyan tree where he had sought shelter from the mid-day sun. And felt very proud of what they had done!

'"Fancy, telling us that we would be strangers in his country!" the village elders remarked. "Who wants to go north, anyway?" echoed the others. "If he be a man of God," some others jeeringly said, "God ought to look after him. Instead of his going to the banyan tree for its shade, the tree ought to come to him. A man of God, indeed! Just a fraud who wants to be fed by simple folks."

'By now the pilgrim was far from them. But a strange thing happened. The tree under which he had rested began moving before the very eyes of the villagers! It slid across the fields at a great speed in the direction the pilgrim had taken, and soon, one could see, it overtook him and spread its shadow over him.

"The villagers were struck speechless with awe. But something still more surprising was in store. They felt the ground heaving under their feet. And before they knew what was happening, their village seemed to be lifted up from the earth! The cottages, the trees, the streets and lanes, the fields round about, the men, women and children, and the domestic animals—all seemed to be shifted on a magic carpet which was being wafted through the air like a cloud!

"They could hardly believe their eyes. But there it was! Their village was floating in the air like a balloon and was drifting towards the north, in the direction of the Himalayas.

"The village eventually landed somewhere in the very country of the pilgrim they had insulted without any reason!

'If you visit the north country,' Moti-Didi concluded', 'you will find some villages where the people speak the language of the south. They are the children of those who had been unkind to a stranger. And they are now strangers in a strange land....'

V

From Moti-Didi I came to learn very many things not to be found in any book. For example, I learned how the singing chaffinch came to get its crest, how the bear lost its tail, why the bee never drinks the honey of the *mohooa* flowers, what one should do to avoid a mad cow, why the fly is as dangerous as the snake....

Here is one of Moti-Didi's stories:

'There was a very God-fearing Fakir who counted his beads regularly as he praised the Lord. Once he was passing through a barren place where he found nothing but rocks and stones and sand. And there he saw a falcon sitting on the ledge of a rock and tearing a piece of flesh into thin shreds.

'The Fakir wondered what the bird of prey was doing in that barren spot. "Why is it tearing this piece of meat into thin bits?" he asked himself. He looked, and saw that the falcon was feeding a tiny fledgling raven, which looked weak and helpless, and could not open its beak wide enough to take a large morsel of food.

'"This is strange," the Fakir said. "It is strange! A falcon feeding a helpless baby raven! There must be some hidden meaning to it."

'Next day he came back to the same spot to see if the raven was still there, and he found it was; the falcon was feeding it as on the previous day. "It is strange," repeated the Fakir. "Falcons feed on ravens, and this helpless baby raven is being fed by a falcon! Let me see what happens to-morrow."

'On the following day he noticed the same thing. The falcon was feeding the raven as though it were its own little one.

'The Fakir fell on his knees and said: "Now I understand the hidden meaning. Great is the charity of God. A birdling which would die without someone's help is being looked after by a falcon! It has no parents and no neighbours. So God has decided to save it. And at his command the falcon is feeding it. Surely the young raven has greater faith than most men, and thus it is assured of its daily meal. And I am a wicked man, and have not enough faith in the Creator. I roam about, wasting my time searching after my food. But if I were to make myself as helpless as the young raven God would, no doubt, send a falcon or some other bird to feed me....

'"I shall not waste any further time," said the Fakir to himself, and decided to sit down under the ledge of the rock where the falcon was, and there he began to praise the Lord night and day.

'He made no further effort to seek his food and his drink.

'A caravan passed by, and the men of the caravan saw the Fakir sitting under the ledge of the rock. They wondered what he was doing there, and asked him: "Are you sick, old father? Can we do something for you?"

'The Fakir replied: "Go your way and leave me in peace. He that feeds the young raven will feed me. Go away from me. I want to praise the Lord."

'The men of the caravan said: "Don't behave like a baby. If you don't seek after your food, why should God look after it? Is it God's business to take care of all crazy people? At your age you ought to show some sense."

'The Fakir became angry and chased them away; and then went into a secret cave far away from the route of the caravans. And there for three days and three nights he remained without food or drink. He was dying of hunger and thirst. No falcon came to him nor any other bird. No one brought him even the thinnest shred of meat.

'On the third night the Fakir had a dream. In his dream he heard a voice say: "Madman! Is this the way to praise the Lord? An old man like yourself ought to know there is a reason for everything. At your age it is not at all reasonable to behave like a child. God's providence is unlimited. So is his wisdom. God requires that man shall make use of the means and talents he has given him. If you are foolish enough to imitate one of the two birds on the ledge of the rock, at least imitate the falcon and not the raven.

'"Be like the falcon that feeds the raven and not like the helpless birdling that has to be fed."

'This shows, my Little Brother, that we are not to behave foolishly on the pretext that the Lord will feed us. Mere believing is not faith. Your way of living will prove your faith.'

VI

'Moti-Didi,' I asked, 'Moti-Didi! As Mohan has a lotus-shaped bell that sounds like a gong, should I not treat him as a grown-up elephant now? He ought to be able to look after me.'

'Why do you ask this, Little Brother?' said Moti-Didi, and she went on sewing without even looking at me.

'You know, Moti-Didi.' I began, pouting my lips, not knowing that I did this whenever I felt annoyed....

Did Moti-Didi notice it? Or was there something in my voice? She guessed there was something worrying me, and looked up.

'Know what?' she asked. 'Know what, my dear one?'

'Well?' I said hesitatingly. 'You have never let me re-visit the mango-grove since *that* day. May Mohan and I go there to leave some *sandesh*, presents of sweetmeat, for the Great Day?'

'I'll come with you,' Moti-Didi said. 'We will all three go together. That would be nice.'

Her consent so willingly given surprised me. Up till now she had been very strict about this; she would not let me re-visit the spot where the thugs had attacked me. So I thought I might as well explain to her why I wanted to bring some *sandesh* there.

'Moti-Didi,' I began. 'We have Christmas gifts for Peon-Dada, Tommy Dum-Dum's father, for Rani Vabani and for others too. And I thought I might leave something in the mango-grove for those who helped me on that day.'

Moti-Didi nodded assent, but did not say anything. 'I must tell you,' I continued, 'Sardar and his *chelas* were scared by the sound of footfalls coming from the garden. And if I had not heard those steps I would simply have dropped down on the ground like a frightened bulbul. And whose footsteps did I hear? Could it have been the monkeys? Or the peacocks? Or was it the guardian angel of the temple?'

By now Moti-Didi was listening to me very attentively. She stopped sewing.

'Providence is kind to those,' she quietly remarked, 'whom the world maltreats.'

'I thought,' I went on, 'that monkeys were cowardly and peacocks were proud. But now I know I was wrong. What should I have done without them?'

'You were never unkind to them, my Little Brother,' Moti-Didi said. 'You never threw stones at them nor tried to catch their young. So they knew you to be their friend.

'Do you know,' Moti-Didi said after another brief pause, 'I have a bag full of hard peas ready for the peacocks and a sack of nuts for the monkeys? I will take some flowers for the altar of the temple. It is good that you should remember those that helped you.'

'But you won't forget Mohan?' I asked.

'Of course not,' replied Moti-Didi. 'Mohan will have two pancakes instead of one.

'I am going to tell you a fable,' said Moti-Didi as she resumed her sewing. 'It is about Cheel and the ant. It will interest you.

'Cheel, the eagle, can stare at the sun and can see even the tiniest of ants. One day an ant had fallen into a stream, and was on the point of drowning when Cheel saw its plight. He took pity on the poor thing and swooped down to drop a twig just where it was struggling in the water. The ant climbed on the twig and was saved. It was grateful for the help it received.

'On another day the ant noticed that a fowler was taking aim at Cheel and the king of the birds was in grave danger of being shot. He was floating high in the air and there was not a speck of cloud to hide him. What could the ant do to save Cheel? An ant cannot shout, and, even if it could, its call would not have helped Cheel. What did the ant do? It crept up the leg of the fowler and, just as he was going to pull the trigger of his gun, it bit him. The fowler missed his aim and Cheel was saved.

'It is like this, my Little Brother. We are neither too big nor too small to help one another.'

VII

Early in the morning we three went to the mango-grove with our gifts, Moti-Didi, Mohan and I. On our way I sang a song for Moti-Didi, a simple one: *Jadi tor dak sune,* If they answer not thy call.

'What are you going to offer Svenska-Bibi?' asked Moti-Didi. 'Tomorrow is *Barrho-Din,* Christmas Day.'

'It is something in leather.' I said. 'It is called a folder, and it has the signatures of all the children of Our School and of some other people too.'

Then I told her that without Karin, Bheem's uncle, Panditji, Cha-Cha, the Bookbinder and others we could not have offered this present.

'All we did,' I added, 'was to write our names in different scripts.'

'Scripts? What scripts?' Moti-Didi was somewhat surprised. 'You are only a handful and all of you speak Bengali. How many scripts do you know?'

'Between ourselves, we know a lot of scripts,' I replied. 'Just make a guess. Soetomo wrote in Javanese and Tu Fan in Chinese; Mazdoor in Arabic and Ayesha in Persian which is very much like Mazdoor's writing; Bheem in Devanagari and Ram Chand in Gujerati which is like Bheem's writing. Then we had Gurumukhi, Burmese, Sinhalese, Ooriya and Bengali. And Karin has written in Latin script which is the same, she says, that they were using in Rome even before there were circuses.'

'Oh! You surprise me! I shall have to ask Jumbo the Mathematician in Pagla's Parade Circus to count out the scripts for me! Pushkar Ram's Pachyderms won't help me. Neither will Mohan.'

Mohan wriggled his ears. He was happy with his big bell round his neck and did not mind Moti-Didi's joke in the least. He knew that though he could not do any multiplication he was not at all bad at counting. Moti-Didi knew it too; otherwise she would not have asked Mohan to deal with her laundry. Mohan knew exactly how many baskets were to be collected and how many to be delivered.

'How many scripts do you know, Moti-Didi?' I asked her as we walked along.

'I am not a learned woman,' Moti-Didi sighed. 'I know only Bengali and Persian. But you will have to know more, my Little Brother.'

'At Sister Svenska's we were discussing which script is the best,' I said.

'And what did you decide?' asked Moti-Didi. She seemed to be interested in our discussion over different scripts. I told her that Tu Fan said that one cannot write Chinese in any other way except as he did and Soetomo said the same about Javanese....

'Moti-Didi, which language is the best?' I wanted to know.

'That's best which serves you best,' Moti-Didi replied.

'Do you know who first said that?'

After a pause she asked if we had quarrelled over which language was the best.

'No,' I replied. 'But we all wondered why there were so many languages.'

'A garden is beautiful, my Little Brother, because there are many varieties of flowers in it. Let us be glad because there are many. But who will tell me if *champak* is preferable to *hasnuhana*, or if the red rose is better than the frail jasmine? It is the same with languages. That's best for you which pleases you the most.

'Now in the days of Akbar Badshah there was a great quarrel over different languages of our land.

'Akbar Badshah was a great ruler who loved God and his people. He lived seven generations before Rani Nilmani's time. And that was long ago. But his fame lives on as though he died only the other day. He was the Emperor of all Hindusthan, and to his court came ministers from many parts of Firinghisthan, the outside world, to see why he was called "The Great".

'Though Akbar ruled over Hindusthan and all people honoured him, he was not happy, for he found his subjects quarrelling over languages.

'"What's all this quarrel about?" asked the Emperor. "You quarrel about which language is the best? I'll give you the answer. That language is the best for you which helps you to express yourself the best, and which helps others to understand you."

'Then he heard that his answer had not pleased his peoples, and that they were still quarrelling. Each people was saying: "My language is the best, for it tells my thoughts best, and everyone else should speak my language."

'Akbar Badshah said, "God intended that each man should love his mother-tongue best, for it tells each man's thoughts best. So why quarrel? You love your mother, and the other man loves his. There is nothing wrong about it, and nothing to quarrel over."

'This answer did not satisfy his subjects either. They demanded that at the Emperor's court there should be only one language, the best language of all Hindusthan. The men of Bengal said: "Let the court language be Bengali, for it is the sweetest of all tongues in Hindusthan, in fact in the whole world." And the people of Kashmir said: "No, it should be Kashmiri." And the men of Rajasthan, Baluchisthan, Gujerat, Mithila, Orissa, and other places made the same claim. Each people said: "My mother-tongue is the best language, and *it* should be the court language."

'"I'll give you an answer," said the Emperor, "in due course."

'Then he told his ministers that he wanted to build a palace and a city, the like of which could not be found in Hindusthan, nor in Firinghisthan, nor in Turkisthan, nor in Chinisthan. "Indeed!" the Emperor said, "I must build a city at the very spot where the holy man, Shaik Salim, gave me his blessing when I was very unhappy. I want master-builders, master-masons, master-craftsmen, and master-artists from all parts of Hindusthan to go there and work for me."

'And this was done.

'Builders and masons and craftsmen and artists came at the Emperor's command to give their best work. Each vied with the other to show his supreme gifts. And such men had no time to quarrel over language nor anything else; they were busy night and day; they were building the fairest of all cities, the new capital of all Hindusthan, Fatehpur-Sikri the Glorious.

'And the Emperor stayed in a camp in the midst of all these people and there he held his court. And he listened to the talk of his artists and artisans and of his guards and his soldiers, and he noticed that these men coming from all parts of Hindusthan had words common to their different tongues. Though the Emperor could neither read nor write he was more learned, and more wise, than most men. He remembered all that was worth remembering.

'When the building of Fatehpur-Sikri was completed he asked his vizier, the Hindu Raja Todar Mall, to invite all the generals, ministers, peers, pandits, artists, musicians, nautch-girls, workers, soldiers and others to come to listen to him. It was a great gathering of people, of men and women from all parts of the Empire.

'And he spoke to them and thanked them all and asked for God's blessing on them. When he had finished he asked:

'"Have you understood me? Or do you want my address to be translated?"

'And they all answered that they had understood him because he had spoken in their mother-tongue.

'"The language in which I have spoken is the language of my camp," the Emperor said. "It is made like the mosaic artists and artisans have made on the floor of my palace. I have seen them take little bits of stones and polish them, and put these pieces in different patterns till the whole mosaic is formed.

'"I asked myself, if a piece of precious jade could speak, what would it say? The piece of jade would say, no doubt, 'I am the most precious of all stones. What have I in common with the blue *neela,* or with the dark-veined onyx?' And if a piece of *neela* could talk, would it not say the same thing?

"What has a blue *neela* in common with the orange sardonyx or the pale jade or with the red carnelian? Is not *neela* more precious than all these? And I would hear the same if all the other stones had the gift of speech. Each would claim its own unique supremacy.

'"But,' the Emperor continued, "when the mosaic is finished all these diverse stones are in perfect harmony with their neighbours. None of them can possibly claim to be better than the rest. All of them blend to please the eye and fulfil the purpose of the artist.

'"In the same way I have made this new language in which I have just spoken. It is made of words common to all the tongues widely spoken in the Empire. It will be understood wherever my rule extends. *This* will be the language of my Court. You may call it Urdu, the language of the camp. Or you may call it the language of the Empire, *Hindi*, if you like. Or *Hindusthani*, if you will.

'"I have given you a common language...."'

VIII

On our way back Mohan seemed to be uneasy. He was sniffing the air and grunting from time to time.

'What is wrong with Mohan?' I asked. 'Moti-Didi, why is Mohan grunting?'

'There seems to be something evil floating in the atmosphere,' replied Moti-Didi rather thoughtfully. 'Let us hurry back home.'

When we passed the sandal-maker's place we found his shop closed. This surprised me most.

There were the two pitchers of water on each side of his shop entrance, and the two coconuts on the top of the pitchers; festoons of coloured paper were hanging over the doorway, and the two banana plants were standing behind the pitchers. Everything looked as it should be at a shop entrance on a day of festivity. But why were the shutters drawn?

In Rani Nilmani's Estate shopkeepers did not celebrate their holidays by shutting up their doors and windows. A holiday meant a day of fasting or of feasting.

'What has happened, Moti-Didi?' I inquired. 'Christmas Eve is for rejoicing. On such a day of festivity people do not close their shops, do they?'

'No, they don't,' Moti-Didi agreed. 'They put on their best dress and call on each other with gifts of oranges. They make everything look nice and tidy. Only they do not like buying and selling on a holy day.'

Mohan began sniffing the air once more, and I saw a number of policemen with red turbans on their heads marching in a file in the distance; they were rushing towards the dockyards.

'Where are they going so fast?' I wondered.

IX

We did not return home, but found shelter in Rani Vabani's palace. Most of the people round about had trickled in there all through the morning when Moti-Didi and I were in the mango-grove with Mohan.

The dock area was on fire. Calcutta was in the grip of a large-scale communal riot. The trouble had started in a brawl between some hooligans, and had then blazed into a general fight between Hindus and Moslems in the industrial areas. In some residential districts mob-rule had begun; and the looting and the carnage made no distinction between Hindus and Moslems.

Gurkhas with loaded guns and drawn *kukris*, large-bladed knives, and units of military police were using the Rani Vabani's palace grounds as their headquarters. Some of them, I noticed, were crouching behind clumps of trees, challenging whoever passed their way, and searching passers-by to find if they carried any hidden arms. Near the signal boxes by the Canal there were khaki-clad military policemen as well as the red-turbaned and white-uniformed ordinary policemen with long brass-knobbed *lathis,* heavy sticks.

I was put in a room where there were other children. Moti-Didi went to another part of the palace. She was to help the doctors who were tending the wounded.

Through the window I could see that the ambulance cars were bringing people covered with blood and mud. There was one ambulance with its sides battered in. It was being pushed out of the way. No one was taken out of it. An English police officer in blue uniform got out of a car, half of which seemed to be charred; two policemen also came out, one supporting the other. One of them looked like Gani's father; his white uniform was spattered with blood.

We saw the wounded, some walking in and some being carried. And the dead were brought in too. We saw also a tall man on a stretcher. He was tossing his head from side to side. He had no arms, for they had been hacked off. But he was not crying.

No, the wounded did not cry. They only groaned when they were being hurriedly carried from the gate to the portico.

We saw Svenska-Bibi in a white overall helping a Sikh out of a yellow taxi. He had a dead boy in his arms.

We did not see Karin. Where was she?

There was something sinister and oppressive in the air. It seemed to weigh us all down, and none of us dared even whisper, let alone talk or cry. We did not know how long we were going to be there, in that room overlooking the gate, the fields and the canals. We had lost all sense of time. We had not the slightest idea when the hideous procession of mangled bodies—of the living and the dead—would come to an end. We could not make out when or why the riot had started, nor what the rioters wanted.

Our throats were parched. Our tears had dried up. All of us shivered, though it was not at all cold.

It was a beautiful December morning, crystal clear, cloudless and warm, such as only the Tropic of Cancer knows in winter.

A confused clamour reached our ears, like the sound of flood waters when the dykes break, or the tumult of the rising tide in the Bengal Bay. It did not in the least resemble many human voices mingled together as in a great gathering, but sounded like a strange medley of savage cries from terrified beasts. Only it was not shrill. It was deep. It was frightening. More terrifying than anything I had ever heard.

It was like a warning coming from beyond the horizon. Was it the beginning of the blast of Doom?

From time to time clangs of fire engines and ambulance cars, rat-a-tats of gunfire, and hootings of foghorns could be heard above this uproar.

A smell of burning wood and tar soon filled the air and made my nostrils tingle, and a pall of smoke floating up from the dock area blackened the atmosphere and made my eyes smart. And the sun hid his face as though shamed by what he had seen. It was darkness at noon though the morning had been so bright and so lovely.

Why did the riot start? Whom did it profit? The Hindus? The Moslems? The Sikhs? Or the Parsees? Or anyone else?

But, thank heavens, it came to an abrupt end. By two o'clock in the afternoon it was 'All Clear.' A death-like stillness suddenly fell. And this seemed at first almost as forbidding as the lull before the burst of a tornado.

A house divided against itself must fall. Was the crash coming?

Did the angels weep? Did the demons laugh? What was this human folly?

'To avert Doom,' the Thunderer counselled, 'practise Charity, Restraint, and Piety.' Did the angels, the demons, and the mortals recall that?

But that evening the sunset was painted in colours rarely seen in a December sky. Did the clouds alone remember that it was Christmas Eve?

X

Had a stranger passed through Rani Nilmani's Estate towards four in the afternoon he would have found our 'Sleepy Hollow' looking outwardly the same as it had always been. Yet it was not quite the same.

The sandal-maker's brother-in-law as well as one of his apprentices were among the severely wounded; and Panditji had a nasty cut from a knife-thrust. Compared with other areas, however, we were extremely lucky.

Unaffected by the events of the morning and of the midday, some of us children went to Our School to listen to the prayer meeting of Tommy Dum-Dum's father, and to help Karin distribute the Christmas presents.

~

The sound of babbling voices from the bank of the Canal where the *neem* tree stood reached my ears as I approached the school.

They were asking Karin to lead them once again in the chorus about the ant with which all stories end.

> Here my story endeth.
> And the lettuce withereth.
> 'Lettuce, why dost thou fade?'
> 'Because the goat is on my wake.'
> 'Goat, why art thou on his wake?'
>
> 'Wife, why dost thou him starve?'
> 'Because the baby doth wail.'
> 'Baby, why dost thou wail?'
> 'Because the ant doth bite.'
> 'Ant, why dost thou bite?'
> 'There's fun in biting.
> And fun in hiding.'
>
> The ant biteth and the baby waileth,
> And here my story endeth.
> Fie on you, Ant! Fie on you!
> The story endeth only for you.

'Karin has just finished a story,' I explained to Ayesha. I had overtaken her on my way as she was toddling along. 'Whenever a story is finished, Moti-Didi has told me, all children sing this chorus about the ant.'

'Do you know why?' asked Ayesha.

I didn't, and I told Ayesha that I would consult Moti-Didi about it. But I could not finish my sentence, for joyous greetings from Karin and others interrupted me.

'Here they come,' 'Here come the last two,' 'The Green Fawn and the Wild Gazelle....'

Ayesha was the 'Green Fawn' because she was in green *pajamas*, and green was her favourite colour, and I was the 'Wild Gazelle' because of my unruly curls.

Both Ayesha and I wanted Karin to begin another story so that we too could repeat the magic formula about the ant. Karin had a look inside the school hall, and as Tommy Dum-Dum's father was not yet ready for the prayer-meeting, she decided to tell us something new.

'This time I am going to give you a tale in a riddle,' she said.

'I like riddles,' said Ayesha, clapping her hands.

'Once there was a great king called Rajah Vikramaditya at Ujjain. He was like Akbar Badsah. He loved his people and his people loved him in return, and called him simply Vikram.

'One day a rich man came to Vikram's court and said: "Rajah, I am a wealthy merchant, and I want to be your Minister. You have many about you who are no good. There is one fellow called Kalidasa in your court. He has written a poem about a cloud! What good is he to you? There is another courtier who says that he has found the value of zero. And what good is he? What is the value of a mere cipher? Just emptiness, mere nothing.... It is no good having such courtiers round about you. Make me your chief courtier and I shall put everyone in his proper place and get rid of all the good-for-nothings."

'At last Rajah Vikram stopped him with the question: "Now tell me, what good are you?"

'And the man replied: "Apart from being wealthy, I can see through useless people. For I understand men better than others, and that is the reason of my success in business."

'"Is that so?" Rajah Vikram said. "Then come back at midnight and we shall go out for a stroll and test your knowledge."

'After midnight Rajah Vikram and the wealthy man went out for a walk. It was a dark night and very windy and cold. The wealthy man did not relish the idea of being out late; but what could he do? The king wanted to test his knowledge, and therefore he had to accompany the king.

'They soon found themselves on the bank of the Sipra River, and there was a fuller beating pieces of cotton cloth in the river.

'"Is it on purpose, my friend," the Rajah asked the fuller, "you are just at the right spot?"

'"Can it be otherwise?" answered the fuller. "The zero line is no accident."

'"You have twenty-four?" Vikram questioned. "Do you need even these six?"

'"For my thirty-two," the fuller replied, "I know what I want."

'"And the far?" asked Vikram.

'"The far is now pretty near,' was the strange reply of the fuller.

'"Would you pluck a goose?" the Rajah inquired. '"Readily," replied the fuller. "I'll pluck its plumes and send it back to you?"

'"Good luck, my friend,' said the king. "There will soon be one for you." And he returned to his palace with his companion.

'On his way back the king asked the wealthy man: "Do you now understand the value of zero? It has kept at least one man very busy, even after midnight."

'"How?" replied the king's companion. "I could not make any sense out of your conversation with that fuller. You talked in riddles with that fellow. What has zero got to do with him?"

'"You are the man," said the king, "who claimed to have the power of understanding men. You insulted my courtiers who have made me as immortal as Skanda, Alexander or the Chief Captain of Heaven. And even now you do not know the meaning of the zero? If you do not bring back to me the meaning of my talk with the fuller by the time the sun rises, you will be judged by my *kotoahl,* the chief magistrate, for slander. And I am afraid my courtiers will demand of you a heavy fine. They may even succeed in securing for you the punishment of exile! I am sorry; but unless you bring me back the meaning of the riddle soon you are lost. I can't offer you any reprieve.... Now leave me in peace till sunrise."

'The wealthy man was very upset. He struck his forehead and called himself a fool. But that did not help him to understand the meaning of the talk the king had with the fuller. So he decided to return to the bank of the Sipra River and seek the busy fuller's help.

'As he was a wealthy man he thought that the fuller would be impressed by his wealth and also by the fact that only a short while ago he was with the king at the very spot where the fuller was working.

'But he found the fuller not in the least accommodating.

'"Leave me alone," the fuller grumbled. "If you don't understand simple things what business had you to ask Rajah Vikram to make you a courtier? Go away and leave me in peace. I am a very busy man. I have no time to waste on you. Your wealth does not concern me."

'"Do you understand?" the wealthy man whimpered. "I shall be ruined. I shall lose face if I do not find an answer to the riddle. If I come to be condemned by the chief magistrate, where shall I hide my shame? Look, here is my purse; it contains a large sum—I offer it to you as your fee if you help me out of my difficulty...."

""That's good," replied the fuller as he took the contents of the purse as his fee. "Now you know the answer to the last riddle. You are the goose Rajah Vikram proposed to send to me. You have been plucked and plumed. You may now return to the royal court. And tell him how you have found the answer."

"'But what about the other riddles?" asked the man.

""They are equally simple for an intelligent man," replied the fuller. "The king said that I ought to rest after midnight; I should have at least six hours' respite during each twenty-four, and I told him that I have thirty-two teeth. That is to say that I am in good health, and I know when to rest and when to work for my own advantage. In the dark the king did not notice if he was talking to an old man or to a young one. So I told him that the far end of my life was pretty near. This solves the riddle 'The far is pretty near.' As for the first question of the king, my answer was equally clear. My place of work is well known as it is on the zero of the map ... the zero of the meridian of the earth, you should know, passes through Ujjain by this bank of the Sipra River where I work...."'

Karin could not finish her story. For the sound of singing now came from the school hall.

XI

The school hall was full of people, all of whom looked like Tommy Dum-Dum's father.

'How can Tommy know who is his father?' Ayesha asked in a whisper.

And to tell you the truth, I did not know the answer. Tommy lived opposite to Moti-Didi's cottage, and I met his father very often. Yet I could not say if he was the man on Tommy's right or on his left. This puzzle has for ever remained unsolved.

The prayer meeting was conducted in a simple way. Tommy Dum-Dum's father and his friends praised the Lord just as Sister Svenska did—by singing. Only they sang in English, Karin told us.

I could judge they sang much more beautifully than we did. At times their voices rose and at times fell. It was wonderful. It was more moving than anything we had ever heard. It was rich and deep. Its very beauty made me feel like crying.

'What are they singing, Karin?' we asked, in a whisper, more than once.

'They are singing simple songs,' Karin whispered back. 'I shall tell you later what they mean.'

Deep river, my home is over Jordan.
Deep river, Lord, I want to cross over into camp-ground.
Deep river, my home is over Jordan.
Deep river, Lord, I want to cross over into camp-ground.

Swing low, sweet chariot,
Comin' for to carry me home!
Swing low, sweet chariot,
Comin' for to carry me home.

I looked over Jordan
What did I see,
A band of angels,
Comin' after me
Comin' for to carry me home.

Who started it? I have not the slightest recollection. Perhaps I had not noticed it. It must have been one of the elders. But ere long we all joined in.

We were shedding tears in silence, we who in the midst of the pain and suffering of the riots had no tears in our eyes.

The prayer meeting ended and the school hall emptied. But we stayed on where we were in the porch. We did not want to move. We had, for the time being, lost all interest in everything. The echoes of strange melodies were ringing in our ears, and our hearts were heavy.

'They want to die,' someone murmured. 'They want to go home. But they can't. So they will drown themselves in a deep river.'

'Why can't they go home?' I asked in a whisper. Perhaps in the back of my mind the story of Mr. Senapati of Siam still lingered.

'Can't they go back home because they have praised the Lord with songs?' Heera wondered.

'Is singing sweet songs on a holy day a bad thing?' I asked myself.

'An impious crime is never forgiven,' I recalled my parents saying. 'Whether you are five or fifty, it does not matter. You will be punished....

'The Yavana Rajah of Megara had two sons. His eldest son got killed while hunting and the younger one came to break this sad news to the father when he was in the temple of God the Law-giver. The Rajah noticed that in rushing into the place of worship the distracted younger prince had knocked some logs from the altar. This was a sacrilege. Therefore the surviving heir to the throne was judged on the spot! And the Rajah killed him by striking him hard on the head with one of the fallen logs.... A sacrilege can never be forgiven.'

'Why can't they go back home?' I asked again.

'They can't go home,' one of the older girls said, 'because there is a deep river between them and their home. They will all be drowned.'

It needed all the art of persuasion on Karin's part to convince us that Tommy Dum-Dum's father and his friends were not thinking of drowning themselves in the Jordan.

'You will see Tommy Dum-Dum's father,' Karin assured us, 'if you bring his present to him. You will see he is taking out his banjo and Tommy's drum. He must be getting ready to celebrate the Great Day....'

But somehow we did not want to be comforted.

~

We had not shed a single tear when we saw the dead and the dying, and now we were crying bitterly.

Did we really believe that Tommy Dum-Dum's father and his fellows were going to get drowned on their way home across the Jordan?

Perhaps we persuaded ourselves at that moment that this was the reason.

In my heart of hearts I knew, however, that it could not possibly have been the real cause of our tears.

We sobbed because we could not help it. We wept, we knew not why.

XII

There was a heated discussion at the bookbinder's shop.

It was tacitly understood that no one should refer to the ugly events of the riot. My surprise was therefore all the greater when

I found that the debate was veering towards the very subject which was taboo!

Panditji's left arm was in a sling. He seemed to be excited, and looked ashen and much older than he was a few days ago when I last saw him.

His opponent was the young student from the College Square. He had a pile of pamphlets in red covers which all had the same title: *The Red Lantern.*

'... Chaos is necessary for the birth of a star,' the young student was saying. 'This is the view of a great philosopher, who saw through the fraud of organized religion. What do you mean by sacrilege? You don't believe in Christianity! Why should Christmas Eve or Christmas be holy? This business of holiness is a dead weight round the neck of Young India....'

'Young man,' Panditji was trying to interrupt the student, 'young man....'

Panditji's efforts were in vain.

'You won't touch any food prepared by a Christian!' the student continued. 'And you accept the holy day of the Christians. Is it not hypocrisy? If there were a God he would not allow hypocrites to roam about all over India.'

'Young man,' Panditji began, 'whenever people meet in prayer to adore the Creator they perform an act of holiness. If many people set apart a special day for worship, that day is holy for you and me as well as for them.'

'You may talk for yourself,' the student retorted in a rude tone, 'but not a single university student will swallow this holiness stuff. The old fogeys have fooled us long enough. And if you think God Almighty will be delighted or distressed with Man's doings you are mistaken! Why should a man be more important than an ant or a gnat to the Creator...?'

'Young man,' said Panditji, 'it is for *our* sake, for *our* own salvation, that we observe holy days. It is not for God's sake. Whenever a large concourse of people pray they confer a benefit on all, on others as well as on themselves.'

'Well, Panditji,' the student burst out, 'if that is so, then why celebrate the Great Day, *Barrho Din,* once a year? Why not have the Christmas prayer concourses every day or every other day?'

'That's a good suggestion,' someone remarked. The student beamed with delight. He thought he had produced a crushing argument against our Panditji.

'Overwhelming emotions are like floods,' Panditji explained. 'If they occurred frequently they would make all life impossible.... In the *Puranas,* it is said....'

The student did not listen any more to Panditji's remarks. He never cared for the stories from the *Puranas,* the ancient epics. He got up, cleared his throat noisily and spat on the ground to show his profound disgust at this turn in Panditji's arguments. Then he walked out without giving his parting salutation to anyone.

He forgot to take with him his bundle of pamphlets, *The Red Lantern....*

~

'Urvashi,' our Panditji concluded, 'the Divine Urvashi is Beauty Incarnate, and she is the hand-maiden of the Immortals. They alone can gaze upon her undismayed. Her matchless brilliance surpasses the tremulous splendour of lightning. If any mortal were to come across Urvashi unawares and did not shut his eyes immediately, he would be struck with blindness. Urvashi is elusive...

'Yet it is the quest for Urvashi, the search for Beauty, that is to say, which is the main purpose of human life. It alone distinguishes a man from an ape, from a gnat, from an ant, and from an elephant. Beauty like lightning tempers the steel but it burns up the dross. A vision of Beauty is the same as a glimpse of the Sublime. It creates an emotional upheaval. Man is incapable of facing the sublime without being overwhelmed. The greater the intensity of his experience, the greater is his emotional upheaval....'

~

Was it this upsurge of soul-stirring emotions which we found too difficult to bear as we listened to the Negro spirituals? And was that why we broke down?

Perhaps that is why all music is proscribed in the homes of Bheem, Mazdoor, and others.

Perhaps it was a good thing that Tommy Dum-Dum's father and his friends did not hold their prayer meetings too often. For not only we children, but the grown-ups, too, were greatly moved as they sang. They had tears in their eyes. And by the time they left the school building they, too, were sobbing helplessly.

'Have they ever heard of Urvashi, Beauty Incarnate?' I have often asked myself this question since that Christmas Eve. Urvashi, I recall Panditji saying, is capable of every form: a cloister for the monk, a fane for idols, a song for the poet, a pasture for gazelles....

XIII

I have heard the song of the crested finches and of the speckled bulbuls; they sing beautifully. I have seen the sheen of the crescent moon in the silver pool; it, too, is beautiful. The kingfisher on the wing and the dragon-fly among the lotuses; these are beautiful, too. So is the sound of lapping waters and of the distant temple bells.

I know the midsummer hush on parched plains, and the roar of the thunder as the monsoon breaks. I have seen the arch of the rainbow and the waves of ripening corn; the falcon flying high in the air, and the dainty glass-fishes frolicking among the reeds; the flight of the white cranes against the sable clouds and the fireflies flitting among the bamboos; new leaves trembling, peacocks dancing and gazelles leaping; sleeping babes at their mothers' bosoms; the shooting stars—and the rush of mighty waters....

I have watched from the Tiger Hill the dawn paint in vermilion the Himalayan snows, and at Diamond Harbour the golden gyres of the sunset fuse and mellow into the night's opal gloom; the lightning flashes and the Seven Great Planets in their course; the rain-washed fields, the windswept heath, and the wayward village road; the morning dew on the rose; the jasmines and *mohooas* in spring, and the red moon of autumn behind the palms....

The perfume of the weeping nyctanthes has thrilled me. So has the caress of a loving hand; the feel of the marble polished by the fountain, and the touch of the swan's down; the smell of the new-mown hay, and the fleetness of the swift-footed horse....

All these have been visions of glory to me.

These were, however, familiar to many a child of Bengal.

But the exquisite music of those singers from a land beyond the seas brought me something new. Its melody revealed a beauty hitherto unknown. It was overwhelming; it was redeeming; it was sublime.

'Perhaps,' I mused, 'I caught a glimpse of the hem of the garments of the Divine Urvashi as I listened to those strange songs sung in a strange tongue. The dazzling beauty of Urvashi's skirt nearly blinded me and filled my eyes with tears. It made me breathless. It overpowered me. I cried because I felt so helpless....'

Others might have had the same feeling. And that was why they, too, sobbed that Christmas Eve when the angels wept and the demons laughed, and a blue moon floated in a smoke-laden sky, and some men remembered the birth of the Child....